AF519900

Praise for the book

The book engrosses you and transports you to the beautiful Lolab Valley in Kashmir ripped apart time and again by violence and bloodshed.

—Mumbai Mirror

The nerve tingling tale of battles between soldiers and terrorists is interspersed with the narrative of love in all its complex shades.

—The Tribune

This is the first combat book written in India, by a Spetsnaz, *a special forces officer who knows the Kashmir Ops the way it really is—no frills, no arm chair theory—straight from the hip. You can smell the cordite and the fear and most important you can get into the head of the enemy!*

Great read specially if you want to know what the fuck is going on in Kashmir.

—Prahlad Kakkar, a man with many hats

The aroma of deodar trees mixes with the acrid odour of gunpowder in this taut adventure story set in Kashmir. The drama is gripping, the characters finely-etched and the plotting authentic. But even as his characters engage in a good-versus-evil battle to the death, Sapru sensitively shows his reader how Kashmir is a tragedy not just for Kashmiris, but equally for the Indian soldier and the Pakistan-backed mercenary.

—Ravindra Kumar, Editor, *The Statesman*

Though his first novel, Abhay shows class of a seasoned writer. Descriptions of terrain, actions, emotions, drama, and violence keep you spell-bound. The tragic reality of Kashmir is so well articulated through this gripping drama, it is guaranteed to win your rapt attention from beginning to end.

—Lt Gen PC Katoch, PVSM, UYSM, AVSM, SC
(Retd)-Parachute Regiment

IN THE VALLEY OF SHADOWS

IN THE VALLEY OF SHADOWS

Abhay Narayan Sapru

Served in the Special Forces, Indian Army

CHLOROPHYLL

First published 2011

This is a work of fiction and any resemblance to any living or dead person or events or places will be entirely co-incidental.

ISBN 978-81-8328-184-3

Published by
Wisdom Tree,
4779/23, Ansari Road,
Darya Ganj, New Delhi-2
Ph.: 23247966/67/68
wisdomtreebooks@gmail.com

Printed in India at Print Perfect

This book is dedicated to:
The Indian Special Forces, whose profession I had the privilege of following.
My late Father (Colonel Sahib) for showing me the way.
My late Mother for silently bearing the disappearances from time to time.
All ex-comrades in arms: my gratitude and thanks for the good times and bad.
Little Ary—May you follow the romance.

'Agar firdous barrui-e-zameen ast,
Hamin ast-o-hamin-ast-o-hamin ast...'
'If there be paradise on earth,
It is here, it is here, it is here...'.

—Urfi

'If a thousand beings like me are annihilated,
what does it matter?
Allah won't have any fewer warriors with wounded hearts!
If my passion is madness, Allah knows I have a reason.
I am a slave to a cause, which has a million drum and standards.'

—Anonymous Mujahidin

'We are the pilgrims, master we shall go
All ways a little further it may be.
Beyond the last blue mountain barred with snow,
Across the angry and the glimmering sea.'

—James Elroy Flecker

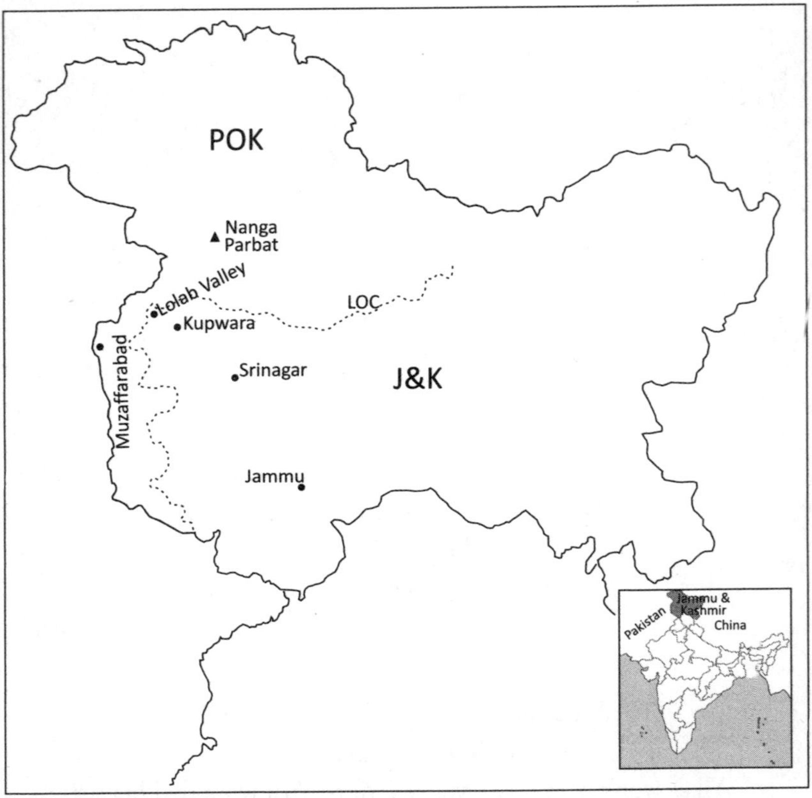

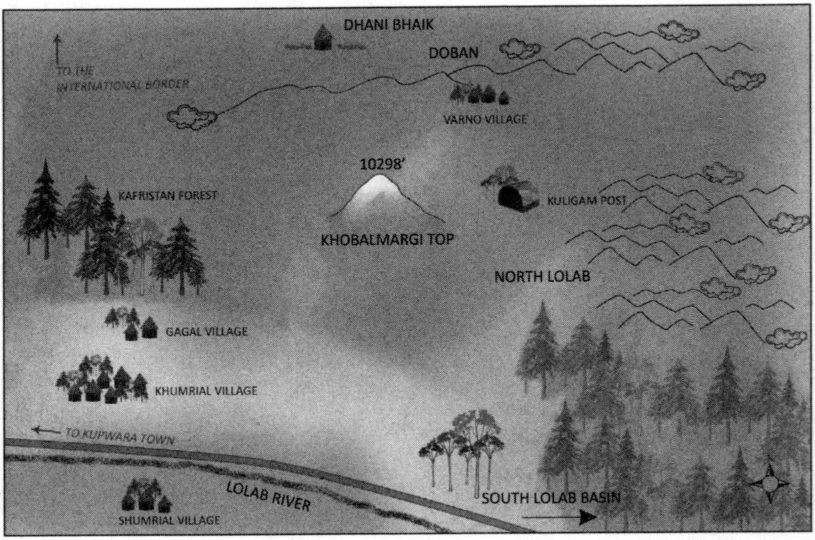

Maps for representational purpose only. Not to scale.

Preface

There is a dry wind blowing through the East, and the parched grasses wait the spark. And the wind is blowing towards the Indian border. Whence comes that wind, think you?

—John Buchan

A MASSIVE STORM was raging on the mountain. There was relentless rain and thunder, and forked lightning split the sky from end to end so often, that it charged the atmosphere with static electricity—the kind that made your hair stand on end and suddenly converted an innocently exposed iron surface, into a conductor. There was an ominous hiss in the air because of the highly charged particles and it was one of those nights when umbrellas, rifle barrels and radio antennae needed to be covered, or the owner ran the risk of grievous harm. It was Nature at its destructive best. A sensible man, on such an occasion, seeks the comfort and safety of home. But sense and soldiering often don't go hand in hand; in fact, in a Special Force outfit, it is taught that it is precisely this kind of bad weather that is ideal for surprise and one often hears the remark that 'a dark night and inclement weather is a commando's best friend'.

On such a night then, in the summer of 1996, I was out with a group of men on a mission to raid a militant hideout, somewhere on a mountain in the Lolab Valley in north Kashmir. As we crested the three thousand-metre high top sometime during first light, the rain had exhausted itself and it promised to be a crisp, clear day. I called for a halt. As I sat wet and shivering, munching my puri and gazing over the valley across Zulu Gali (as it was called by the army), my sight was held by a range of very high snow clad mountains. Puffs of white clouds floated on their shoulders and the tops glowed pink in the early morning light. From amongst them, rose a towering giant, head and shoulder above the rest.

'Nanga Parbat, *jenab*[1], the local Gujjar guide said, reading my thoughts. 'That's in Gilgit, Pakistan.'

I allowed my soul to briefly rise and soar over the valleys and mountains, for the distance to the big mountain did not look too much. I wondered about the kind of fundamentalist adventurers who came from there, calling themselves the mujahidin—'soldiers of God.' Was it purely religion that drove them to take such risks, or some sort of rustic romance with soldiering? I wished times had been different and I could have just continued walking. Gilgit, Hunza, Chitral—names on a map never to visit. It was then that I had a strong urge to capture in a tale, the people, the place and the setting of this so-called *Jehad-e-Kashmir.*[2]

In the context of time and place, most of the main characters of the novel are based on real life people; Sher Khan and his cronies definitely are, but it is fair to say that it was a common code-name used by foreign militants across the valley, and often when one Sher Khan perished, another would step into his shoes. This particular Sher Khan and I inhabited the same valley for a year or so. Proud of his Pashtun lineage to the point of arrogance,

---

[1] A polite way of addressing a senior in age or experience.
[2] Holy war in Kashmir.

cocky about his fighting ability with complete conviction in his cause and effort, Sher Khan displayed utter disdain for the Hindu race. He was a perfect example of some of the leaders who ran and managed the Jehad for the Pakistani establishment in Kashmir. I often heard him speaking to cadres on the radio and did manage to engage him in conversation a couple of times, but these were always brief and ended with, 'We'll meet in the field, *fauji* bhai.'

In fact, on one occasion where we managed to eliminate a few members of his group, Sher Khan came onto the Brigade radio network. He was furious and kept challenging the army. By the time we turned up at the decided rendezvous, he had left. Along with most of his cronies, he was killed barely a kilometre and a half away from the divisional headquarter. They had spent the night planning mischief in a house very close to the road. It was the wrong choice for a meeting place and no sentry was posted for an early warning. They had been sitting down for breakfast at ten in the morning when the army cordoned off the house. His arrogant over-confidence finally got him an unmarked grave.

I had often believed that perhaps the foreign militants were romantics and adventurers in their own rustic sort of a way. Well, they were not. Some were in it for economic reasons, but the majority were malevolent, religious zealots in varying degrees, with a very narrow vision to life. They had a kind of esprit de corps, as any good fighting unit should have, but with loose group affiliations. When cornered, they invariably fought well and to the bitter end, their attitude towards death often bordering on indifference.

The description of the Bedouin by T E Lawrence, in his book *The Seven Pillars of Wisdom,* may well have been written for the average foreign Muslim fighter in Kashmir: 'They were a limited, narrow-minded people, whose inert intellects lay fallow in incurious resignation. Their imaginations were vivid, not creative.'

He further describes them as having a belief, 'almost mathematical in its limitations and repellent, in its unsympathetic form'.

The history they had been taught in the madrasas was limited and covered only the parts that embellished Muslim glory. Most of the senior cadres I spoke to on the radio, had never heard of Ranjit Singh, the Sikh, who ruled from Lahore, or for that matter, knew much about the British rule. However, they had heard of Mahmud Gori and Timurlane. They were very proud of having defeated the Russians in Afghanistan and believed it was just a matter of time before America and India would 'scatter to the winds' as well.

On our side, like any professional army, we produced the usual good and bad officers and men. There were the brave and the sensitive, malingers and cowards. All sorts made the rank and file who did their tour of duty in Kashmir. But by and large, contrary to what has been written by the media about army atrocities, it was and still is a well disciplined and good army. I would be surprised to see any army in the world in similar circumstances, deployed for years in combat duty, acquit themselves better. There were men in my battalion who had served in Siachen or Nagaland (both operational areas), who were then posted to Kashmir. By the time they left, some had done a great many years in active combat zones.

In my own case, I spent nearly four years in an operational area from Nagaland in the east, to Kashmir, before stepping out to environs that were more peaceful. That is a long time to be moving constantly and living out of a rucksack. Anything over a year in a highly volatile, insurgency environment, living rough and existing on the edge, can be enervating and mentally exhausting. The raison d'être to serve in the profession is questioned.

The locals, while initially being responsible for the encouragement of such a militant movement, end up the victims of a tragic play, where the script has gone horribly awry. Most of the villagers I spoke to in the hinterland, though accepting that it was their fault (defending that in the maelstrom of events, one lost the ability to reason), remained indecisive to what they wanted—pro India, pro Pakistan or *aazadi*. This indecisiveness or sitting on the fence and waiting for a winner before taking a call, became one of the reasons for their prolonged misery.

It would not be too much of an exaggeration to say that the core of the story is true, to the extent that some of the dramatic personae mentioned (with names changed for obvious reasons) existed, and the incidents did happen. Javed Jabbar, the local militant commander, did cross paths with Sher Khan and was punished for it. The incident is narrated in exactly the way it happened, having been picked up from militant radio intercepts and later from villagers. Javed was finally shot by us, but not before he managed a fatal casualty on our side.

Having blown up an improvised explosive device under the brigade commander's vehicle on the Lolab-Kupwara road and having earned his days salary, Javed, walked into our ambush very near his village. Typical of his cunning nature, he was moving cross-country instead of using the village paths, and ended up behind the ambush rather than in the killing ground, resulting in a sharp, fierce fire fight.

Likewise, certain conversations with militants, dialogues between various protagonists, along with geographical places are non-fictional as well.

Sometime in 2010, the battalion was operating in the valley and a fighting patrol of ours clashed with a heavily armed group of mujahidin in the Haphruda forests. In the initial stage of the fight, we suffered some serious fatalities and the militant group thereafter splintered and broke contact. The CO pitched camp on site and refused to pull out till he had squared the account. The running fight over the next three days resulted eventually in the elimination of the entire group of twelve militants.

A few of us who had retired made a trip up to Kashmir to be with the men. A spin across to the Lolab Valley was most disappointing. While the road had improved, human habitation had impinged further up the mountain and the valley looked more populated. But that was not the crux of the disappointment we felt for our old hunting ground, and it took a while for us to realise what was missing. The palpable nervous excitement, the tiny knot of fear, the sharpness of the senses, the overwhelming feeling of being alive, was all gone. 'The old order changeth'. While insurgency levels had fallen significantly, it was the absence of any militant chatter on the radio which conveyed most ostensibly the drastic change. Both the army and militants, we were told, now preferred using mobile telephones and the good old fashioned IED and sniping by the adversary had become a dying art.

But '*fikar nai sir*', said the CO looking at our crestfallen faces, all is not lost for the future generation, for while the age old modus operandi of guerrilla warfare may be obsolete, the quality of the enemy has improved significantly. We now invariably face—the fedayeen.

The story is basically a narrative of the life and times of the myriad characters that having been thrown together, exist in an insecure, hostile surrounding, plagued by years of militancy. Along the way, arrive the gamut of human emotions, flaws, dilemmas, love and betrayal, within the army, the locals and the militants.

If the tale is violent, then all I can say is, so was the environment where I spent my youth.

Abhay Narayan Sapru

Lohsar–1, Pakistani Post (POK)

April 1995 | Friday-2200 hrs

There's a time to make war and a time to make peace.
You can't have war and peace. So you make a silent war.
—Yitzak Rabin

The night was impenetrable and only the faint whiteness in the starlight was visible where the snow still sat between trees. The moon in its fourth quarter was expected to make a feeble appearance in the early hours of morning, provided the omnipresent clouds didn't threaten snow. A light breeze blew across the valley and picked up the only thing it could: a chill from the snow around. There was an ominous quiet except for the faint sound of the river below. Those acquainted with the area knew that the silence was just a façade and a very thin line separated the tranquil hush from unimaginable violence; a violence that could erupt regularly and often, very suddenly.

The nooks and corners of the forest were alive. The nightlife in the undergrowth was active, and little lives scurried about on important errands. An owl screeched for its mate, diving at a scrawny mountain rat, which hesitated at its hole, out on a first foray outside after hibernation. The owl missed and flew back to a branch shrieking in frustration, his big eyes rotating in surprise at having missed such an easy target. The rat scratched its ears, unaware of how close death had come, remaining motionless, still mustering enough courage for an excursion. A black bear ambled across silently, ignoring the rat and heading towards the rocks, where he was sure to receive the first rays of the sun. To the uninitiated, the whisper of the forest was unheard; it was quieter than a church after Sunday mass.

As he sat on the ground, Sher Khan leaned his back against the mud wall of the bunker, zipped up his jacket, folded his knees and bunched his shoulders against the chill that crept up his spine from the cold wall. He closed his eyes and tried to sleep, but his mind was exploding with thought. He looked in the direction of the other five men in the group, seated in a line against the wall, but could only make out their silhouettes in the darkness. He was certain none of them could sleep either. Anyone who could manage to sleep under the circumstances, he thought, either was an incurable optimist, or a fool, or had Allah's promise for longevity. It wasn't everyday that one crossed a heavily defended border into another country.

Sher Khan knew that none of the men there, were any of the above. He had known three of the men personally, for many years. Malik and Gul, apart from being relatives from his mother's side, were his classmates from the same madrasa in Muzzafarabad. The three had played together as kids and fought together as young men. The third man, Sheswar, was from Gilgit and had met the trio in a militant training camp in Muzzafarabad. They were a team and the four had been through *jahanum*[3] and back many times in Afghanistan.

[3] Hell

In fact they had reached a stage, where they addressed each other by their radio call signs even under normal circumstances. Real names had long been forgotten, lost on the battlefields of Afghanistan. Sher Khan didn't know the other two men, but they were professional Gujjar guides, who earned a living by taking *tracks* (groups) across the Line of Control (LOC). He had been told they were the best in their trade. They had done it many times; they had to be good. Just to reinforce his views that none could sleep, he called to Malik in a whisper.

'*Haan*, Sheru bhai,' replied a gruff voice from the darkness.

'Just checking you are carrying the spare batteries for the radio? I am told the Indian army has put a ban on the sale of pencil batteries across,' replied Sher Khan, smiling in the darkness, happy that faith in his men was rightly reposed and knowing men like Malik were too seasoned to forget such details. More men like these and we would change the map of Pakistan, or the world for that matter, he thought.

'Plenty of stock. You think I would forget our lifeline, Sheru bhai?' answered Malik. 'Must cross today; it has been a long wait and you can't have a better day to cross. Its *jumma,*[4] continued Malik.

'I know,' replied Sher Khan. 'Look at the night. Can't even see my hands in front of my face. Reminds me of the night we ambushed the Russian convoy in Kandahar.'

They had spent uncomfortable four nights at the post. Major Imtiaz Ali was the post commander of the Baluch Company, in charge of the operations in that area along the LOC. While his company headquarters were at Lohsar with one platoon, both his remaining platoon posts were on either side of his

[4] Friday (Prayer day for Muslims.)

position, running along the ridgeline—a typical, volatile border deployment.

The major had been particularly hostile in his reception towards the mujahidin, now being hosted by the company. Perhaps, thought Sher Khan, he was jealous the mujahidin had more combat experience and were doing all the fighting, while the Pakistani regular army manned the posts. Or maybe he wanted to be back in the comfort and safety of his wife's bed. Too soft for this game, thought Sher Khan. The soldiers at the post had been more open in their admiration, shaking hands and telling them to kill many Indian dogs.

The first night they had gone down to the river, when a shooting star had blazed a silver trail across the sky. The Gujjar guides had bought them back to the post. It was a bad omen, they said. The second day Malik was running an upset stomach and the guides refused again, saying they would take only fit men. The third night they had started the climb after crossing the river, when once again the guides had turned them back. The lead guide had stood watching a hole in the snow next to a tree, and then had gone down on his knees and smelt it.

'Some body has urinated,' he had said. 'The Indians must have come down for a check, they are still around; they are alert.' That was all he said, by way of explanation. Sher Khan couldn't figure out how the guide had seen the tiny hole in the darkness and the fading footprints in the snow behind. Perhaps he knew which trees the Indians used regularly as a pee spot.

Sher Khan had started wondering if the guide was scared, and was trying to postpone the crossing. They had decided to take a day's break, and wait for *jumma.* After all, they were fighting in the name of Allah and he would protect them on his day.

Major Imtiaz Ali had spent a year at this god-forsaken post and he had no taste for this sort of a life. He was a short, fair man, with an emerging bulge along his waist, quite noticeable in his tight uniform—a result, in his line of work, of having spent more time behind a desk than in the field. He was a career soldier, more comfortable in an operations room, where he could impress his seniors in his articulate English, a benefit of a good public school education. In his pocket, he carried the joining letter he had just received from the Commandant Staff College Quetta, welcoming him to the course. He was meant for higher command he thought, not waste his talent running mujahidin and signing leave certificates and pay rolls for the men.

The rations were another bone of contention. He was showing additional manpower in the records, to cater to the floating population of militants, but he knew from experience that once the snow melted and the passes opened, his company would be like a transit camp. The orders were very clear: complete assistance and support was to be provided to the mujahidin. After all, they were washing the dirty linen of the Pakistani army, and that too, at the Indian ghats.

So far, he had survived and performed reasonably well. It was a high-pressure, sensitive job and performance was evaluated on the success of infiltration achieved. He thanked Allah for saving him from carrying out some of the stupid orders one could expect to receive, in this kind of a hostile environment. He remembered Asim, his course mate, a company commander like him, of a Punjab Battalion on the next spur. He had been tasked to carry out a retaliatory attack on an Indian post across his defenses. The retaliation had come too soon.

The Indians had been expecting it, and had given him the bad news with all the might they had. It had been a complete disaster. Sixteen bodies had been carried down the mountain. Poor Asim was one of them.

Tactically his post was at a disadvantage. The Indian post overlooked it, from across the river, higher up on a spur. Twice, in an exchange of fire, the Indians had used rockets, causing casualties in the post and on both occasions, he had been on leave. 'Two more months to survive, and *Insha' Allah*[5], I'll be out of this hellhole on my way to Quetta', thought Major Ali as he stepped out to talk to the guides.

The major found the mujahidin offering namaz. He waited for them to finish, peering into the darkness towards where the Indian post was. He wondered what was happening there. The men got up and the senior guide walked up to talk to the major. His name was Rashid, but he was popularly known on either sides of the border, by his pet name Hathkarhi, or handcuffs.

Hathkarhi had been apprehended thrice by the Indians and had managed to escape each time. The last time round, he had crossed back into Pakistan, still wearing the steel handcuffs the Indians had decided to use, knowing his past record for escaping. At the Pakistani post, it had been a problem to cut them. He had finally got rid of the handcuffs, but the name had stuck. He was a veteran of thirty-two border crossings and what he did not know about the trade, was not worth knowing. Professionally the major had a very high regard for him, not because of the regular spirit he displayed at doing the Houdini trick with the Indians, but more because he had an unblemished record at border crossings. The major owed his earning a good report, to him.

'You know the plan Hathkarhi,' spoke the major, 'I'll give you one hour to cross the river and at exactly twelve, my post will open up. There's still snow and the Indians don't expect the crossings to start so early. You stand a good chance. May Allah be with you, *Fi Amanillah*.

[5] God willing.

'*Fi Amanillah jenab*,' replied Hathkarhi, shaking hands with the major and turning to the men who had hoisted their rucksacks and weapons on, and were standing in line, waiting for his instructions. 'From now on,' he told the waiting men, 'till I hand you over to the launch commander in Doban, you are under my command. You will do exactly what I tell you to do. I will be leading and Saleem, the other guide, will bring up the rear. In case we are intercepted, stay together and engage. I have already briefed you about the Indian army's deployment.

After the border post, there is another line of defensive troops, followed finally by more troops operating in the town and villages. The first two deployments are my concern. Keep your ears and eyes open and don't break contact in the darkness.' Then turning, he silently disappeared into the darkness between the trees.

It took a moment for Sher Khan to realise that Hathkarhi was not there. Wrenching himself away from the safety of the post, he followed the guide down, on his way to the river. He didn't feel the need to say a farewell to the major—he abhorred his kind. In any case, the major had already turned and disappeared inside his bunker. He was more worried about his dinner getting cold.

Machhal Sector (North Kashmir, India)

April 1995 | Friday-2200 hrs

Life not put to the test is not worth living.

—Epictetus

Lieutenant Sonny Nambiar put his pen down and looked at the platoon's senior *subedar*[1] with an irritated frown. He didn't like being disturbed when he was writing his stock of letters and this one was to his girlfriend in Kochi. He needed to choose his words carefully, to put it across gently. She had to take a decision. In his situation, it was easier to start a war than find a girlfriend. It was a make or break situation.

'Yes, sahib,' he answered. 'Have the boys had dinner?' He noticed the senior *subedar* had had his quota of booze and his eyes were red. Nambiar didn't know how to handle the situation; he was too young in the battalion. He didn't like it that the senior Junior Commissioned Officer (JCO) of the platoon got high every night. It set a bad example and portrayed him as a weak officer. Though, he had to agree, that the man was correct in his conduct, physically tough and did his job well. But his most irritating

[1] Junior Commisioned officer in the Indian army.

habit, thought Nambiar, was that he was constantly teaching him how to run the platoon.

'You have to do the guard check, sahib,' the *subedar* said. 'Battalion headquarters have passed information that the infiltration might start anytime.'

'Well, I know what I have to do, sahib,' replied Nambiar, trying not to show his irritation, as he got up to leave, picking up his balaclava.

What he didn't know was that the company commander had briefed the senior JCO to look after the kid and teach him all about being a good officer and a good soldier. That was how the Indian army worked.

The platoon post was on one of the many spurs that ran down to the river, from the main ridgeline at an altitude of nearly two thousand metres. The river here formed the line of demarcation between the two nations. A thick jungle of deodar covered the slopes, limiting visibility to ten metres. A section post of ten men had been thrown forward, further down the spur, to act as an early warning. The terrain was such that it necessitated deployment along spurs and ridges, with height domination, at times, being the only consideration for deployment. This often necessitated an uncomfortable proximity to the enemy post. The closeness of isolated section posts to each other, also made them vulnerable to the odd assault that both warring armies launched on each other from time to time, to occupy ground or inflict casualties.

Namby, as he was known in the battalion, walked out of the small bunker, which served as his bedroom and stood, briefly looking across, towards the Pakistani post, wondering what the Baluch Company commander was doing now. Probably in his bed somewhere in the rear, he reasoned. The Pakistani officer lived and conducted himself like an officer, he had been told, unlike his Indian counterpart who was always supposed to be doing what his men were expected to do. Bullshit, he thought. There was a time to lead and a time to relax and this was all the more important with this acute officer shortage that the army kept talking about. He had a chat with the sentries, peered over the sandbag walls into black emptiness, heard the reassuring roar of the river below and decided that all sounds and sights were familiar. No infiltration would take place today; the snow was still too thick on the ground.

'Is the ambush party out covering the nala, Bajrang sahib?' he asked the *subedar*, over his shoulder, turning and retracing his steps back to the bunker.

'Yes, sahib,' replied the *subedar*. 'Ten men under Havildar Ram Kishan. I have told them to roll back by six in the morning.'

'Good,' said Nambiar, getting back into his sleeping bag. He increased the light of the paraffin lamp, picked up the letter he was writing to his girlfriend and chewed the end of the pen, thinking of the right words. He never got down to putting pen to paper, as the next instant, hell temporarily shifted location to his platoon post. His girlfriend was the last thing on his mind as Lieutenant Nambiar rushed out of his bunker. In any case, it was too late; she had already walked out on him, with a computer salesman.

Hathkarhi took them down to the river at a fast pace. He didn't seem to be too careful, breaking twigs and passing loud instructions to Saleem from time to time. It made Sher Khan wonder if they had picked the right man, because otherwise, it seemed to be a cakewalk across. The moment the party crossed the river a sudden change came over Hathkarhi. He stopped and looked up at the dark mountain for a long time, wrinkling his nose and smelling the air, like a woman would, for perfumes in a shop. Sher Khan guessed he was trying to get into the Indian post commander's mind, though he did suspect that Hathkarhi in all probability had enough information about the troops at the post and was taking a decision accordingly. He hoped that they would not be asked to turn back a fourth time.

Then like a gun dog latching on to the smell of some hidden game, Hathkarhi pointed towards a spur coming down from the main ridgeline.

'That's where the Indian post is,' whispered Sher Khan in alarm.

'That's where they least expect us,' replied Hathkarhi, with a chuckle.

For some time they climbed straight up towards the Indian post, leaving the nala to the right. Suddenly, Hathkarhi stopped and looked down towards the nala. Sher Khan followed his gaze, wondering what the man could see in the pitch-black. It was like being wrapped in a shroud, with a blindfold. For a brief moment, Sher Khan couldn't make out anything in the inky blackness and then he saw the cigarette, glowing in the darkness, like some one-eyed mythological beast. A little later the beast moved, as the cigarette was passed around. Hathkarhi smiled to himself in the darkness. The rest was easy, he thought. He showed the position to the others.

'Ambush party,' he whispered, taking a watch out from his pocket to check the time. 'We wait here for the fireworks to start.'

Sher Khan realised what the guide was up to. He was cutting through the gap between the post and the ambush, covering the nala. Clever, he thought, his admiration for the guide going up a notch or two. He heard a steady throbbing sound in the darkness and placed a worried hand over his heart, embarrassed that the others would hear the ruckus it was creating. With relief he realised that the sound was the throb of the generator, coming from the Indian position. Wouldn't like to be a guide, he thought, for a paltry twenty thousand rupees. The risks were far too high. Next instant, the silence of the place and his thoughts,was interrupted, as the black veil of the jungle was torn to shreds by the sound of a hundred rifles blazing away in unison.

'Now!' said Hathkarhi, swinging right from the original course and moving forward at a fast pace. 'Follow me and don't break contact!'

Major Imtiaz Ali stood outside, next to the machine gun bunker, hands on his hips, like a belly dancer poised before the last act, watching the tracer bullets stitch a fiery path across the river towards the Indian position. He knew from experience, that the Indians would take a few minutes for the orders to go up and down before returning fire. He stood his ground, watching the tracers weave an intricate design in the sky and wondering, if a glowing tracer bullet hurt you more than a normal one.

Major Ali never did arrive at the conclusion to his question, or for his staff college course at Quetta for that matter, as the first rocket from the Indian position blew off his head. They buried him headless. He was the only casualty the Pakistanis had that day.

Lieutenant Nambiar may have had his own views about soldiering, but you needed a clever mind to propound views and the strength of conviction to put those views to the test. Namby wasn't short on either quality. Life, he believed, should be put to a test, or it was not worth living. In college, he excelled at sports and aspired to follow his father into the Foreign Service. But a trip to Mhow with his classmate, whose father was in the army and serving at the Infantry School, changed the course of his life. He was fascinated by what he saw of the profession and the army.

It was an immediate choice for young Nambiar, much against the wishes of his parents.

He knew they had a defensive reactive strategy. Fire when you are fired at, use the same weapons, and take the same reaction time. He had decided he wouldn't wait for orders to return fire. If they fired on him, he would reciprocate with interest. The last time, he recalled, the Pakistanis had opened up because they had lost a cricket match against India. They had caught him by surprise. Probably the Pakistani Company commander was a cricket enthusiast, he thought, while he had never played cricket. That was why there was so much passion in their firing. Crazy, he thought. Like kids fighting over who was going to bat first, though most of the time, he realised, the Pakis did.

The border was so sensitive that if a fly went across with India written on it and sat on a Pakistani plate of dal, or the other way round they would exchange fire, for violation of air space. Well, the last time they had done it over a dog, so the fly example was not too much of an exaggeration. It was a Pakistani dog, he recalled, attached to their cookhouse that had strayed across to the Indian post. 'Wants a change of taste sahib, possibly our rations are better than the Pakistani's,' the men had joked. A Pakistani soldier had come under a white flag and requested that the dog be returned immediately. Namby had sent him back after two days, with a message tied around his neck, that much to the reluctance of the dog he was being returned, as they already had many uninvited mad Pakistani dogs overstaying, and the next one would be returned dead.

Briefly, Namby had been tempted to pack the dog with explosives and blow him up with a remote controlled detonating device, at the Pakistani post. But then he had felt sorry for the dog and he didn't have explosives either. Anyway, the Pakistanis had thanked him for returning their dog by firing at his post for two hours. Namby couldn't understand why they had done it. No bloody sense of humour, he thought. Possibly, they were slighted at his message, or maybe they thought the dog had lost weight during his stay with the Indians, or perhaps it was just another Pakistani way of showing gratitude.

Namby remembered attending his course mate's marriage in Etah, where the bridegroom's family who were rich landed Thakurs, had fired a substantial amount of ammunition from the assortment of weapons the *baraat*[2] had carried. They had practically blown the roof of the tent away in their joy. For an orthodox Mallu Brahmin, the experience had come as a shock. Maybe the Pakistanis were over joyous at receiving their beloved dog back after two days of Indian captivity and like the Thakurs had decided to fire their cannons in celebration. Except, unlike the Thakurs, they had a target to aim at.

He had learnt his lesson and learnt it the hard way. Reprisal must be immediate and with equal ferocity. He had changed the drills thereafter. No starting from smaller weapons and increasing the calibre. His orders to the men were: react fast, start with a big weapon and stay big. The rocket launcher had been placed, with the sights fixed at the Pakistani machine gun bunker.

Even before the first Pakistani tracers had started drumming their staccato beat of death on the sandbag walls of the Indian post, the eighty four millimeter high explosive anti tank warhead often used for bunker busting, was meeting the Pakistani tracers, crossing into Pakistan over the river. Heading towards the Pakistani position, it sought the unfortunate man, whose name seemed to have been written on it, when the round was cast.

---

[2] Bridegroom's wedding procession

Namby never really got to know how well his tactics had paid off. However, the next day he went out for an inspection of his platoon's defended locality, for he was certain from the volume of fire he received from the Pakis, that an infiltration had been attempted.

Barely three hundred yards downhill from where his ambush party had been sitting, he came across several boot marks in the snow. You didn't have to be Sherlock Homes to figure out where the group of men had huddled in the lee of an overhanging rock, waiting for the fireworks to start, before cutting across the ambush party and pushing inwards. One boot mark stood out for its size and the deep intricate pattern of the sole. Now that is an expensive snow boot, thought Namby. Clearly a big, bad guy. Pity, he got through. The problem was now of the troops in the rear. At least he had managed to give them a bad scare, he thought with a wry smile. At the moment though, the tough part was to inform the battalion headquarters about the missed chance.

Namby got through to the adjutant in the rear on the radio. Major Kohli was a superseded, dull officer who specialised in unit politics and behind the desk operations.

'Well!' said Major Kohli sounding incredulous on being told about the infiltration. 'Not possible,' he kept muttering in the mouthpiece, as his dull mind tried to grasp what Namby was saying. 'Not possible,' he said again louder, as if it was a complete breach of faith on the part of the Pakis to allow infiltration before the snow had melted sufficiently and in defiance of the infiltration pattern worked out by the Indian army.

'Check the foot prints again, Namby,' he retorted. 'You are possibly mistaking bear pugmarks, for boots.'

'Negative, Sir,' replied Namby, losing his patience with the man,

'Not unless this bear is wearing size twelve, expensive snow boots and carrying a heavy rucksack on his shoulder.'

Namby heard a faint giggle at the other end, the sarcasm clearly lost on the dull Kohli imagining Paki bears wearing snow boots and romping around in order to confuse the Indian army.

North Lolab Valley

INDIA | (THREE DAYS LATER)-0700 HRS

The spring at its source may be turned with a twig;
When it's grown to a river it cannot be crossed by an elephant.

—Sadi

IT TOOK SHER Khan and party three nights to reach their destination—the Lolab Valley. They had covered the distance at night, resting and lying low during daylight. They had walked through the Hajibal forest to the junction of Gishatwar, leaving Baghtor and Kalzahwan to the left. They had hit Shalpat Bhaik on the second night, sometime after midnight. A few hours' rest and they had marched again, arriving at Pathardhari Bhaik, at a height of thirty-five hundred metres. Hathkarhi decided to wait the night out on the ridgeline, before rolling down to the Doban Valley in the morning to make contact with the launch commander who would be responsible for their further arrangements.

Sher Khan took a deep breath and rubbed sleep out of his eyes. He felt exhausted and his shoulders ached from the heavy weight he was carrying. None of them had eaten much and Hathkarhi had forbidden lighting a fire to make tea. Sher Khan stood there and had his first look at the valley of Kashmir, at the snow-clad mountains in the backdrop, down the thickly forested ridgeline, to the sweep of the distant North Lolab plains—the cluster of poplar trees and the shimmer of tin roofs in the sunlight. Ribbons of white smoke from the chimneys, hanging in uncertainty, waiting for a current to give direction, indicated where a village stood. Barren brown fields crackled in anticipation of activity and dusty white tracks intersecting each other, formed bizarre designs. He sat down against a tree, lit a cigarette and inhaled deeply. He wondered now for the first time, about his life and the mission he had been sent to accomplish.

He was born Shenawaz Muhammad Khan at a small village close to the town of Muzzafarabad in Pakistan Occupied Kashmir (POK). His father had been a soldier in the Pakistan army's Northern Light Infantry and had been discharged from the army on medical grounds because of a lung infection he developed while serving in the Siachen Glacier. He survived now on the small army pension that he received and an even smaller patch of land that he owned. Shenawaz studied up until the ninth class at the local madrasa in his village and then dropped out to look after his ailing father whose health was deteriorating every day and eating into the family's tiny income.

On one of his trips to Muzzafarabad, he had noticed the different *Tanzeem*[1] offices, with a crowd of eager youngsters queuing outside for recruitment.

'They are off to Afghanistan for jehad,' the old shopkeeper told Shenawaz. 'Look at them, are we not proud of such fine men upholding the right of Islam. Allah! have mercy on the Russkies.'

Shenewaz had often heard the *mulla*[2] during the *jumma* sermons

---

[1] Islamic religious organisation.
[2] A Muslim priest.

at the mosque extolling the contributions of the mujahidin in Afghanistan. He remembered what the *mulla* had said in his last sermon.

'The first pillar is the *shahada*[3], the profession of faith: There is no god but god, and Muhammad is the messenger of God. Allah moulded man into a most noble image and in the end he shall reduce him to the lowest of the low—all except the believers who do good works—for them, there shall be boundless rewards. For only those who die in conflict with the unbelievers, will find *jannat*[4]. In the *hadith*[5], Muhammad says, shall I not tell you the peak of the matter, its pillar and topmost part? The peak of the matter is Islam, the pillar is prayer; and its topmost part is jehad.'

The sermon had left a deep impression on young Shenawaz and he decided that he wanted to be a mujahidin—a holy warrior, and a pious *musalman*. More importantly, it would fetch him some money to look after his ailing father. With his two classmates Mansur and Gulam he walked into the Harkat-ul-Ansar office and offered his services. He was eighteen years old. They were given a twenty-one day course of intensive training in firing, weapon handling, radio telephony and explosives and just before his nineteenth birthday, Shenawaz Muhammad Khan found himself operating in Afghanistan with a band of seasoned fighters from as far away as the United Kingdom.

The camaraderie and brotherhood was amazing amongst the mujahidin, considering there were people from all over the world. Shenewaz had found his calling; he had discovered his raison d'être.

It was here in Afghanistan that his ISI handlers discovered him;

[3] Muslim declaration of belief in the oneness of Allah.
[4] Heaven
[5] Narrations concerning the words/deeds of the prophet.

he earned himself the nickname Sher Khan and more importantly he discovered himself. At twenty-three, he was the leader of his own group, leading independent operations with a motley group of mujahidin from various parts of the world. Sher Khan had arrived as a guerilla leader. He was present in the taking of Kabul and later in the battle for Mazar-e-sharif. He was sent back to Pakistan a couple of times by the *Tanzeem* to motivate and recruit youngsters, for other than being an experienced fighter he was also a powerful orator. Everywhere he went, his emotional speeches moved the crowd to fervent chanting and an overwhelming support for jehad followed.

The ISI handlers saw in him the makings of an archetypal guerilla leader. Physically, Sher Khan stood well over six feet. He was slim, broad shouldered, with a straight long nose on a long face, and he sported a flowing beard, with shoulder length hair. He was an imposing personality, the kind who would stand out in any crowd. Born in more peaceful and opportunistic surroundings, Sher Khan could have been the toast of the modelling circuit. Here, his looks helped to make him a natural leader of men. He was a product of his surroundings, a victim of circumstances.

Temperamentally, Sher Khan was happy, thriftless and aggressive, essential qualities in a man, who has to lead and remain under intense pressure of survival for long periods in a combat environment. Bellicose by nature, the product of his Pashtun ancestry and a fundamental, religious upbringing made him a formidable fighter. He was courteous and full of personal vanity. His thoughts were focused on day to day events and moments and he suffered little from any stress about the future or regrets of the past.

The ISI had a talented natural for the job. They groomed him further.

The Russians were withdrawing out of Afghanistan and Sher Khan came back to Pakistan more convinced in the invincibility of the Mujahidin. He was married at twenty-five to his uncle's daughter and for a brief period, enjoyed the comforts of matrimonial bliss. But his was not a nature to be shackled to domestic responsibility for too long. He made another trip to Afghanistan, fighting for the Taliban in their push against Mahsood and then came back in the winter only to discover that his father had died and that his presence at home was urgently required.

He stayed home for the next two years trying to eke out a living from his meager land and doing odd jobs. But Sher Khan was doing something he wasn't born for. He was shrinking as a man; a part of him was dying slowly every day. This was when he got a call to join back the Harkat-ul-Ansar. For the devil's flame now burnt in the valley of Kashmir, and men like Sher Khan were required to fan the flame into a fire. He was two months away from his thirty-fourth birthday when he crossed into India.

Sher Khan lit another cigarette and admired the tranquil, beautiful scene below. It was difficult to imagine violence in a place like this. Hunger was making his stomach rumble loudly. He recalled Colonel Aslam of the ISI, briefing him about his task.

'We lost the last man Hamza bhai, call sign—HB, who was handling the show in the Lolab and Rajwarh area,' said the colonel. 'There is utter confusion. Incorrect situation reports are being sent, funds are being siphoned off and the movement seems to be losing momentum. Quite a few local mujahidin have surrendered. We want you to go in there and take stock of the situation, rally the different groups and regain the initiative we have lost. Lolab Valley is important to us in this game.'

'Understand,' Colonel Aslam had paused for emphasis, looking him straight in the eye, 'you are there to make people fight, not to fight yourself. So don't get provoked into proving any points to anybody. You have done your share.' The colonel had ended by quoting Sadi:

The spring at its source may be turned with a twig;
When it's grown to a river it cannot be crossed by an elephant.

'Similarly,' he had smiled, as if the entire wisdom of jehad, was encompassed in the couplet, 'turn the tide now, Sher Khan, before it turns into a Hindu river in spate, drowning us all in its path.'

Easier said than done, thought Sher Khan, making a tiny hole in the ground, where he shoved the cigarette. He was a careful man, and that was why he wasn't five feet under the ground, like so many of his friends. He firmly believed that no cause was worth dying for stupidly. Slowly he covered the hole with earth and then leaned back resting his head on his rucksack. Within seconds, Sher Khan was fast asleep.

Somewhere in North Lolab
(0700 HRS)

Noor-e-haq shamma illahi, ko bujha sakta hai kon,
Jiska hami ho khuda, usko mita sakta hai kon?

'Oh, who can extinguish Allah's flame?
And how can you harm anyone,
If Allah stands to protect his name?'

FOR THIRTY-SIX hours, Major Hari Haran watched him, in that remote valley at around three thousand metres. A lone figure with about thirty heads of cattle to give him company. Tirelessly, he would traverse the mountain a hundred times up and down after the animals, his shrill whistle carrying up to them in the still mountain air. In the evening, a fire flickered in his dilapidated *bhaik*[1], where the major could imagine him sitting down alone to a frugal meal. During the night, Harry, as the major was called, had watched him get up a few times to feed wood to the fire which burnt outside the cattle pen, to keep the bears and leopards at bay.

In those thirty-six hours that Harry watched him, nothing

[1] Shepherd's log hut.

suspicious was noticed in the man's mundane existence. Alia Chopan (Chopan is a man who earns his living by taking the village cattle during summers to the heights for grazing) was beyond reproach, leading a life in solitude, forgotten to the rest of the world.

Harry broke the ambush and decided to have a word with him on the way down to camp. Alia was a small, innocuous looking man, emaciated, with an air of sickness about him. His toes were sticking out of torn plastic shoes and a tattered dirty shirt stitched crudely in many places, fluttered in the light breeze about his thin torso, like a loosely fitting flag on a pole. With frightened, big eyes he watched the rest of the column rolling down from the heights.

'You are Alia Chopan?' Harry asked.

'Yes *jenab*,' he hoarsely answered, through dry, cut lips.

'What is this we hear about you supplying rations to the militants?'

The scared, tired eyes exchanged astonished looks with those around him, as if appealing to all against the injustice of such an accusation. Silently he watched, as the men searched his meagre belongings. A couple of kilos of rice, chilli powder and tea leaves were the only possessions he had. His expression of surprise, Harry realised, was genuine. He was too poor to supply anything to anybody.

'This is what you eat?' Harry asked.

'Yes *hazur*.[2] Rice and this green *saag*[3] that grows wild for sabzi and *kahwa*[4]. All I can afford.'

---

[2] Sir.

[3] Green leafy vegetable.

[4] A popular Kashmiri delicacy, hot concoction of cardamoms and almonds and water which keeps the body warm.

'Where's your wife?' continued the major.

'Don't have the money to get married. Which father will give his daughter in marriage to a pauper like me?' he said, looking forlornly at his meagre belongings lying on the ground.

His body search produced a torn plastic wallet, with his identity card, a rupee coin, a doctor's prescription in Urdu saying that he had some sort of a brain problem, a couple of Dispirin tablets and a paper chit, intricately folded, with Arabic letters and numbers.

'What is this?' asked the major, holding up the chit.

'A *Pir*[5] sahib has prescribed a *minnat*[6] for my medical problem.'

'And what problem do you have?'

'Severe headache, *jenab*,' he replied rubbing his forehead. 'Never ceases. It's difficult to work and at times I faint. These tablets the *hakim*[7] sahib prescribed, give a little relief, but there doesn't seem to be any permanent cure.'

'Well not unless you get yourself operated I guess and even then I don't think there is any permanent cure. It's called migraine in English.' Harry described the symptoms, while Alia sat on his haunches, nodding his head and stroking his chin, as only a Gujjar will, in agreement.

Feeling sorry for him, Harry ordered the men to hand over their left over puris to him. Some stale sabzi and pickle followed. Then in a mood of generosity and more as an attempt to reduce weight for the return journey, the tea rations surfaced. Someone donated his torn gloves, another, his old scarf. Harry tipped him some money to buy shoes.

During the entire proceedings, the major noticed Alia Chopan's

---

5 A Muslim saint.
6 Humble entreaty.
7 A practitioner of Ayurvedic medicine.

expression switch from fear, to astonishment, to gratitude and then overwhelmed by his emotions and holding his aching head, he squatted at the major's feet. Harry knew for Alia it was the first experience of kindness and that too, from least expected quarters.

'Alia,' said the major, 'any mujahid information you get must come straight down to our camp at Kuligam.'

'Yes *jenab*,' he mumbled, still dazed at the windfall of events. Then before Harry could get up, he held on to his ankles with both hands.

'No Alia,' chided the major 'You touch only God and your parents' feet. No one else deserves such high respects.'

'Sahib,' interjected one of the men, 'he's not touching your feet, for that's a Hindu custom. He is asking permission to massage your feet. His way of showing gratitude and paying you back.'

A strange way to do so, thought the major. He declined the offer politely. Alia's crestfallen face and the men's clamour to give the poor man a chance to square the account forced Harry to sit down again.

For the next ten minutes, Alia Chopan, with his filthy callous hands, put his heart and soul in the massage, while Harry sat there, feeling rather stupid, with the men looking on, waiting for the sahib to finish his massage.

'Thank you.' said Harry. 'That should suffice for the march back.'

'Did *jenab* like it?' Alia asked expectantly, in Gujjari.

Harry looked deep into his sad black eyes and smiled.

'Yes, Alia,' he answered, ruffling his dirty hair. 'By the oath of Allah, never before, or ever after, will I ever get a massage like this!'

A lopsided, happy smile lit Alia's face.

Kuligam-Army Post
(1915 HRS)

Ghamand Chai na, Tari Chah.
'I am not arrogant, I am cocky.'
—Gurkha saying

MAJOR HARI HARAN entered his post and saw his two company officers smiling at him as they stood outside to receive him. They hadn't had any success for some time and there was a healthy competition between them, as to who would break the jinx.

'No luck, sir,' said Lieutenant Ashutosh Shah, smiling. 'So the bet is still on.'

'Sure kid,' said Harry. 'He who gets the first kill, gets free beer for the month from the other two.'

Ashutosh, or Ash, as he was called in the battalion, was the kid of the company. A small, wiry man, he was twenty-one and always raring to go. A product of a military school, he had been a gymnast at the Military Academy. He came from a humble middle class background, where his parents were schoolteachers at the local central school. Their only dream was to see their son commissioned as an officer in the Army. Harry had met them once, before the unit moved into operations and had seen the silent admiration in their eyes. They absolutely adored their only son.

When out on an operation, the major had to detail a man in the party to keep an eye on the lieutenant sahib. In the heat of action, Ash had a tendency to go berserk, like a misguided missile. Harry had often lectured him on the subtle difference between a brave fighter and an intelligent fighter, quoting Patton that you won a war not by getting yourself killed, but by killing the other bastard. But Ash had only smiled a smile of youth. A smile that had seen no death, loss or injury; a smile that spoke his mind and said—I won't die sir, I can't die, I am too young to die.

'You show me how brave you are, Ash,' Harry had told him, 'when I ask for it. Till then, stay in line. Don't get yourself killed and more importantly, don't get the men under your command killed. In your two-year stay you can't solve the Kashmir problem. Let the others also contribute their two-penny bits.'

But the major knew how futile his lectures were. He had been like Ash as a youngster in Sri Lanka. Every age has a different shade to colour a man's perception. The kid wanted to prove himself, thought the major. And prove himself, he must. It was his prerogative as the senior officer to control Ash and equally as a young officer, it was Ash's prerogative to prove himself. If somebody lost his life or got maimed in the bargain, well, too bad, thought the major. In this business, one traded in lives and didn't prove a point in the same way as an insurance salesman did.

The major looked at the other officer standing there and realised that he couldn't have had a better second-in-command. Captain Bobby Singh was one of those dream officers that the army threw up once in a couple of courses. Steady as a sniper's rifle, thought Harry. A Sikh from Pune, Bobby was built like an athlete, was of medium height, and in his late twenties. To those who met him for the first time, he came across as over bearing, bordering on arrogant. And arrogant he was. It was an arrogance born from being the best. He had been a service cross-country runner, a karate black belt and was exceptionally strong. His entire body language when he walked into a room full of strangers was—come and try me, and if you can't, well, then don't expect me to have too much respect for you.

When roused to ire, Bobby could be like a mountain torrent in spate, difficult to stop and bubbling over with boisterous aggression. Harry was completely the opposite with aggression that would often go unnoticed, submerged under a veneer of outward calm. Bobby's aggression was in the moment and therefore spilled over, uncontrolled, while Harry knew that his own, sustained for a longer time. Harry recalled how in his initial interactions with Bobby, he had noticed the silent challenge in his eyes and was forced to accept the invisible gauntlet if he wanted respect from Bobby. With Bobby, you had to earn your respect. You didn't get it if you were wearing a little more brass than he was, on your shoulders.

They had tested each other in the mountains, or the mountains had tested them. But in the end, Harry knew Bobby would stay in line. Bobby's only irritating habit that Harry was still uncomfortable with, was his tendency to compete. If you did something, Bobby wanted to beat you at it. It just went against Harry's philosophy. If you competed with anyone, it was with yourself. No one else set the standard for you, you set it for yourself, and you were answerable to yourself. But then, that was the quality that made Bobby different. A quality that had driven him to top all his courses and be an excellent officer, on or off the field.

'Bloody waste of time,' said Harry. 'Need to open the account soon, before the colonel starts breathing down my back.

Start praying, gentlemen. The other guy does it five times a day, requesting your demise. Chances are, God might listen to him.'

'*Parva illae*[1], sir,' said Bobby. 'We'll hit something soon. Radio traffic has increased, and there seems to be a lot of movement suddenly. Maybe the militant groups have started arriving with the snow melting on the heights.'

'What are the guys at the LOC doing?' asked Harry. 'They sleep away the nights and we lose ours. Maximum attrition should be at the crossing since obviously we haven't been able to plug the holes. Is the TV working, kid? We need to stay in touch with the world.'

'Reception's not too good...Something to do with the direction of the antennae,' answered Ash. 'Pamela would be a bit of a blur, sir. The essential parts of her anatomy might not be so clear.'

'Well, if Pamela's contours are going to be confused, we might as well stick to the contours of the map. No point watching TV,' replied Harry.

They sat in the evening around the *bukhari*[2], for the weather was still chilly. The major noticed that the distance of the people from the *bukhari*, was directly proportional to the heat it was generating. Through the evening he had noticed, how the *bukhari* had cast a spell on their movement. In its dying throes, the three of them were practically hugging it. As if in answer to Harry's theory, Bobby opened the cover of the *bukhari* to peep in.

'Feel like getting into it,' he said. 'Ash, tell someone to get it kicking. We still got to have our dinner.'

They lapsed into silence, concentrating on a disjointed Pamela and her bevy of babes frolicking in the water on the TV screen.

---

[1] Don't worry (Tamil).
[2] Wood-fired or coal-fed heating device.

Baywatch was probably the most popular serial on TV for the section of the Indian army that slogged it out in the back of beyond. More than the women, it was the picture of fun, happiness, cities and people, which the average soldier related to. *Baywatch* had everything that an Indian soldier didn't. So he escaped into a dream world during that time. Operations, when possible, were planned keeping the day of the serial in mind.

'Switch it off,' said Harry disappointed. 'No point, the tits are getting all mixed up and mutilated with the lines and if you can't see Pam's tits, you might as well not see her at all.'

So they just sat around reading or writing letters. The major was enjoying his rum and pani. A drink was always most satisfying after a hard day's physical work, he realised. The radio was on automatic intercept mode and from time to time it would lock into some frequency—a snatch of conversation in Kashmiri, between militants discussing the day's happenings, or a couple of Gujjar militants cribbing about their life. The chatter of conversation from the radio and the *bukhari* crackling in gleeful heat were the only sounds in the room.

'*Tohedis gamas jenab*,' said a voice in Kashmiri, loud and clear. '*Manaj che, haj police chook.*'

'*Aan haj*,' replied a voice, fainter and breathing hard, as if he was climbing. Then the voice died as he went out of range. The *bukhari* lapsed into silence having burnt itself out, the room fell quiet and the radio started running through the frequencies again, like a petrol metre at a gas station.

None paid any attention. In the Lolab Valley, between eight in the morning and nine in the evening, it was like a one-day international cricket match, thought the major. The commentary would continue till the end of game in the evening, when the score would be declared. How many dogs (soldiers) killed,how many mujahids *shaheed*[3], crackdowns by the army and the commentators' views, sitting in some Pakistani Army post across the border, on the progress of the Jehad.

Generally, the Kashmiri militants were fonder of chatting than the foreign mujahids. Possibly, being locals, they had more to discuss. The major turned his attention to the book he was reading. *The Bear Trap* was written by a Pakistani Brigadier of the ISI, who ran the Afghan desk during the Russian occupation of Afghanistan. The similarity of the conduct of their operation to the one in Kashmir, struck the major. They had just picked up the same template, the same business model and applied it to Kashmir with slight modification, of course. The next instant the three of them were staring at the radio set as a heavy voice filled up the small room like smoke from a freshly lit *bukhari*.

'*Asalaam-walekum*[4], I am Sher Khan,' said the man, his cockiness and authority practically oozing out of the radio. 'I'll be going out on my *daura*[5] of the valley soon. Till then *mohtram*, carry on with whatever you have planned.'

They waited but the man did not come on the air again. Maybe he had switched channels or his radio batteries were low, or maybe high ground or an obstacle of some kind screened him. The three of them exchanged glances. They recognised most of the voices on the net and this was a new one.

'Sounds authoritative. I bet he is the new replacement for good old HB,' said Harry.

'If he is here to stay, we'll surely know in the next few days, sir,'

[3] Martyr
[4] Peace be upon you.
[5] Tour

replied Bobby. 'And before the *bukhari* dies on us, I think we should have our dinner and hit the sack. You know the old soldier saying, sir—get your food and sleep while you can, for who knows when they become a scarcity.'

Doban Valley (North Lolab)
(1400 HRS)

Our life here is truly hellish. Fortunately, my soldiers are very brave and tougher than the enemy. What is more, their private beliefs make it easier to carry out orders which send them to their death. They see only two supernatural outcomes: victory for the faith, or martyrdom. Do you know what the second means? It is to go straight to heaven. There, the houris[1], *God's most beautiful women, will meet them and will satisfy their desires for all eternity. What great happiness!*

—Mustafa Kemal Atatürk

FOR TWENTY-FOUR hours, Sher Khan, Gul and Malik had slept a dead man's sleep, getting up once to have a meal of corn roti and *kadam* [2]. Hathkarhi and Saleem had collected the final instalment of the money that had been promised to them by Sher Khan, as balance payment to be cleared on successful infiltration. They had parted company to return to their village in Sonapindi on the Indian side. While the other two had hit the sack immediately, Sher Khan had spent some time with Ishaq Lone, the local launch commander at Doban, discussing the situation.

The Doban Valley lies northwest of the North Lolab basin and

---

[1] Beautiful, virgin women in heaven.
[2] Cabbage

is approached by a rock-strewn dirt track, which veers off the main Kuligam-Varno road. The track runs for a few kilometres along a mountain stream before entering the forests, as it climbs up to the three villages of Doban, Dharia and Maidan. Sixty-odd houses are all that constitute what the impoverished community of Gujjars, call their home. Meagre land cleared for cultivation and stunted famished cattle are the only source of existence for the Gujjars. Unemployment, illiteracy, proximity to the border and a detailed knowledge of the terrain ensured the villagers' participation in *Jehad-e-Kashmir*. The area produced some fine guide material.

'Well,' said Sher Khan, having walked around the hut, satisfied with the isolated surroundings and the early warning system worked out by Ishaq, in case they were surprised by an army patrol. 'Call all the battalion commanders here for a *salah-mashwara*[3] tomorrow. I would like to introduce myself and the new mujahidin with me and instruct them personally on what is expected from us by our seniors across. Incidentally,' he continued, getting under the quilt, 'if any of them is feeling too lazy to walk the distance, tell them I carry the pay for the month.'

Sher Khan sat in a lotus position on the warm *gaba*[4], with Malik and Gul on either side. The other men sat in front. Sher Khan sized them up. There were eight men. Javid Jabbar controlled the area from Kalaruch in the north to the village of Shumrial in the south, with the town of Kupwara also under his jurisdiction. This was the most important area and other than controlling the frontier town of Kupwara, it also facilitated north-south movement across the river. The chain of mountains was the narrowest at the junction of the twin villages of Khumrial and

[3] Meeting/discussions
[4] Kashmiri Rug

Shumrial, offering consummate cover to cross the road there. Javed was an important spoke in the wheel.

Javed had been a barber before he turned to militancy. He was short, thin with a mean face and shifty eyes. He had an insolent, slimy aura about him, giving the impression that he couldn't be trusted. Cruelty and malevolence ran deep in him—he had a penchant for using a cut-throat razor, a throwback from his previous profession. They said he always carried it in his pocket. Sher Khan took special note of him. He knew trouble when he saw it, for he had spent enough time with the likes of Javed Jabbar.

The other two battalion commanders, Manzoor and Tiger, in charge of south Lolab, looked like steady, senior men, who would toe the line and do as they were told. They were more interested in flattering and fawning and were desperately trying to impress Sher Khan with their achievements. Some of these men were genuinely involved in the Jehad, thought Sher Khan, looking the men over, while for the others, it was just another way of earning a living. Javid Jabbar, he was certain, fell in the latter category.

The politics of economics, he thought, was like any other movement of such a nature, in this part of the world. Sher Khan was not an educated man by the standards of the world, but he was worldly wise. He had spent time with some educated men during his stay in Afghanistan. Omar, his best friend there, had come to fight all the way from Birmingham, in the UK. A graduate, he had been a great eye-opener for Sher Khan. Over a couple of ambushes and raids, they had become close friends.

While for Sher Khan, fighting was a way of life and a source of income, Omar had been completely different. Sher Khan could never understand the so-called romantic Muslim warrior image Omar had of himself. He believed that for a life to be complete, a confrontation with death was necessary. It was Omar who had insisted that Sher Khan should apply for a visa and go back with him to England after they had wrapped up the Afghan embroilment. Sher Khan had readily agreed.

But the war gods don't dance to a mortal's tune. Omar was killed that fall, by a Russian anti-personnel mine. Sixteen people had walked along the same path on the same spot and nothing had happened. Omar had been the seventeenth man and way down in the column. He had nothing to fear and death was the last thing on his mind when the mine exploded. He was dead even before he landed back on the ground and Sher Khan saw his dreams of a trip to *vilayat*[5] blow away with the fading echoes of the explosion. He knew then, that his only chance for a better life, was over with the death of Omar. This was the first time he had suffered a personal loss, for Omar was like a blood brother.

He realised the uncertainty and fragility of life and the mysterious ways Allah chartered each man's destiny. So many mujahidin had died and so many more would go. One day he would also go to his maker, probably unsung and forgotten, like the dead leaves of the mulberry trees blowing in the wind before the onset of the cruel Afghan winter. If Sher Khan was shaken by the death of his friend, he was also convinced of his destiny. Allah had other plans for him. His time had not come yet. After all, he had been the sixteenth man walking ahead of Omar.

'I presume, that you may have been expecting someone to replace HB,' said Sher Khan, addressing the men in Urdu. 'Well, I am the man who has been sent. In the last three months, since HB bhai was martyred, the situation in the Lolab has deteriorated. We have had no success, many mujahid brothers have attained *shahadat*[6], and others are surrendering in droves. You don't fight

[5] Foreign land.

[6] Martyrdom

a jehad like this,' he said, making eye contact with each of them, and raising his voice just a little, to show his disgust. 'And if you think you will win *aazadi* at this rate, then it's a dream only fools can indulge in. Martyrdom is the quality expected from a good mujahid.'

'We have come here,' he continued, looking at the other foreign militants sitting there, who had come as bodyguards with the battalion commanders, 'not because we have been forced to, but because we feel for our Kashmiri brethren. While we, the guest mujahids are prepared to die for the cause, we only ask for your support and commitment for the Jehad, and Insha' Allah, we will see you walk free of the shackles that force you to live under this *zalim mulk*[7].'

It was a stirring speech and Sher Khan knew that the men present there, knew who the boss was. Enough for a first introduction, he realised. Now to set some examples and they would follow like a kite to the first gust of breeze.

'I will be getting in touch with each of you, but first I will go around seeing my area of operation and assessing the ground situation. In the meanwhile, I want you to keep up the morale of the boys under you. It's just a question of who can last longer, between the Indians and us. And before we part brothers, there is something important I need to share. There is a poem, *A Mujahid's Fariyad*[8], which I would like each of you to carry and read to your other brother mujahidin. Make sure that like your code book, it must never fall into the hands of the army.'

Sher Khan pulled out a piece of paper and slowly, in his powerful voice, read out the poem.

---

[7] Oppressive/Cruel country.
[8] Request

Oh Allah! In jannat, if you are watching,
strength to our arms do give.
We fight a jehad in your name; your enemies we have sworn to slain.
So bless and protect us, for the sake of our honour and fame.

For Allah, thou art the merciful and the compassionate.

Oh Allah, do guide us, in our endeavour and aim.
Many a mujahid perished, upholding your holy name.
Do grant your slave one wish;
that he meets you without suffering pain.

For Allah thou art, the merciful and the compassionate.

Oh Allah, we have fought from Hindustan to Spain,
Spreading your message to the world, with blood, sweat and pain.
After a bloody blow to the infidel Christians,
A kafir Hindustan shall we rename.

For Allah, thou art, the merciful and the compassionate.

Oh Allah, the Russians, we scattered yesterday,
Hindustan, we will see, breaking today.
Wherever they threaten the Moslem race,
The wrath of the mujahidin, will they face.

For Allah, thou art, the merciful and the compassionate.

Oh Allah, neither in a masjid,
nor in the shade of our neighbour's wall,
For namaz shall we offer, in the shadows of our mighty swords?
Five times a day we think of you, summer, winter, fall.

For Allah thou art, the merciful and the compassionate.

Oh Allah, at times, I feel weary; my eyes shut to a deep sleep.
Grant your slave the strength,
for first signs of the blossom I do perceive.
The blossoms, oh brothers! Are here to remind,

That fruits can't be far behind.

For Allah thou art, the merciful and the compassionate.

Oh Allah, grant us fateh[9], *only then the lesson to the world be plain.*
Long is the list of shaheeds, *longer the list of kafirs, slain.*
And we have sworn to be your warriors,
At the point of death and pain.

This then Allah, for your jehad, is the mujahid's fariyad.

For Allah thou art, the merciful and the compassionate.

[9] Conquer/win

Army Post—Kuligam (North Lolab)
(2130 HRS)

A skirmish in a border station,
A canter down some dark defile,
Three thousand pounds of education
Drops to a ten rupee jezail.

—Rudyard Kipling

A STEADY RAIN drummed a monotonous beat on the tin roofs, and like a rolling barrage, thunder bombarded the little valley. Lightning cut open the night sky and in the brief flash of light, the soggy leaves of the poplar and walnut trees hung limp and lifeless. The earth was slushy, a frog's delight and the fields submerged with water, ready for the rice plants. Numerous small rivulets had come to life, only to die suddenly, a few hours later, once the rain stopped. Everything was dripping, soggy or filled with water. Water dripped through the tin roof and got under the collar of the sentries' waterproofs. The clothes in trunks were soggy, the rations in the store soggiest. It had to be, it was the wet month of July.

The village of Kuligam is located a kilometre or so inside North Lolab basin. Further north of Kuligam, the valley opens out to accommodate five more villages. A single narrow, metalled road that had seen better days before militancy blew away all thought of repairing it, runs between terraced fields and apple orchards, to the village of Varno, at the end of the valley. Various smaller valleys open into the North Lolab and in two of the larger ones, lie the villages of Ahfan and Rang. Like most villages in North Kashmir, rivulets gush down through the centre of the village to meet the main river flowing at the base of the terraced fields. The valley is at a height of nearly fifteen hundred metres and the ring of mountains around, rise to nearly three thousand metres.

A decrepit, old log cottage, used before as a logging camp by the forest department and now deserted, had been taken over as the company headquarters. Thick deodar logs lying in the compound were used for building perimeter defences. The cottage had three rooms, with an attached dining area and a kitchen. Compared to the modest houses of the villagers around, the cottage was a luxury. A string of mulberry trees formed a natural screen from the road. An experiment to introduce mulberry in the area had been aborted by the forest department when the soil was found to contain too many pests. The stunted trees however, gave a fair amount of fruit for their size during the season. Hordes of birds would then descend, creating a ruckus loud enough to drown out any conversation.

A platoon was ensconced in a disused storeroom across the road looking out towards the open fields, leading to the river, while the third platoon had found quarters in a big two-storey log house about half a kilometre uphill in the Gujjar area of the village. The owner of the house and his entire family had crossed over to Pakistan. Most villages in Kashmir have a clear distinction in the demographic distribution of land. The affluent Kashmiris occupy the initial part of any village and own the more fertile part of the land, while the Gujjars are pushed behind, occupying land at the periphery of the village, generally shoved further up the mountain.

Major Hari Haran tucked himself further into the sleeping bag and looked out of the window, at the soggy night. He heard the incessant patter of rain on the tin roof and the distinct pat of the single drops, leaking from the roof and collecting in the various vessels strewn around the room. A thin, tangled branch from the rose creeper outside had managed to creep into the room, perhaps in an attempt to escape the battering of the rain, and a couple of leaves now dangled in front of Harry. He liked it, it gave him a feeling of being outdoors. The best sleep one could get, he realised, was when nice and cosy in a sleeping bag, under a tin roof or in a tent while it rained.

Briefly, Harry allowed himself to ruminate over the events of the last couple of months. His company had managed a few surrenders of some of the local militants and recovered a substantial amount of arms and ammunition from a cache, but no kills so far. Maybe the militants were keeping clear of his area because of aggressive area domination and possibly, he decided, it wouldn't be a bad idea to keep a low profile and allow them freedom within his domain, hitting them when they were off guard. Very much like big game hunting, he reasoned. Beat the drums in one part of the jungle and drive the game to the guns. Except that here, the game was far more dangerous. One never knew who was stalking whom and when the hunter became the hunted. Well, I must discuss the plan tomorrow with the other two, he decided, checking his watch and adjusting the pillow. Think of women and sleep, he told himself, before the rain stopped and the effect of the booze wore off.

Harry had barely graduated from the conscious to the semi-conscious state, when loud knocking woke him.

'Somebody has come in from the rain to see you, sahib,' said the sentry. 'He nearly got shot in the bargain. Says his name is Alia Chopan and that you would remember him.'

Harry remembered him, the impoverished Gujjar who suffered from migraines and had massaged his feet a couple of months back. To come in this weather, at this time, the guy must really have a problem. Probably looking for another windfall, thought Harry. Alia Chopan was escorted onto the veranda. He was dripping, like the leaves outside and shivering as though a current ran up and down his thin body. His teeth were chattering loudly. The drenched state had set off his migraine, which was probably now playing Ping-Pong in his head, for the pain jumped from one side of the head to the other. He saw Harry and squatted on the ground with his head between his hands.

'Everything alright, Alia?' asked Harry. 'Not the right time to come to us, you could have got shot in the darkness.'

'*Jenab*, I have come down from the mountain in this weather to inform you about a militant hideout that I know of.'

Harry was suddenly serious, his sleep forgotten in the excitement.

'Get him into my room,' he told the sentry. 'Wake up the other officers and tell them to join me and try and get a hot cup of tea and some dry clothes for this man.'

They sat around with a map spread out on the crude wooden table in the centre, while Alia, squatting on the ground, noisily sipped his tea. The generator had been switched off and the lantern threw grotesque giant shadows on the wooden walls.

'What's the story, Alia?' asked the major.

'*Jenab* they came,' he blurted, his eyes dilating with excitement, the migraine forgotten briefly. 'The mujahids. They were six of them. Four of them were definitely foreigners. There was a tall man who was the leader and one of the mujahids was a *hapshi jenab.*'

'That could be a Sudanese fighter. The locals call anybody dark, a *hapshi,*' interjected Harry, in answer to Ash's inquisitive glance.

'*Jenab,*' continued Alia, 'they came down the mountains in the afternoon and asked me to slaughter one of my sheep and cook a meal for them. Then they sent me down to Varno village with a note to collect rations and batteries. I was thereafter, forced to carry the rations beyond Khobalmarghi, to a spot in the Kafirstan jungles. I didn't see the hideout but I know it's in a cave close by, for I have spent some nights there long ago. If you want, I could take you there *jenab.*'

'What magic did you work on the guy sir,' asked Bobby, 'for the man to come down in this weather?'

'Good PR,' said Harry laughing, 'You just have to be nice to people and things follow on their own. Right gentleman, as I see it, the hideout must be hit tomorrow morning, the sooner the better, before they move out. It's quite a climb and in this weather, I doubt that we can manage it by first light. So that leaves us only the option of driving from here to Z Gali. Once you have the height, then it's just a two hour walk to Khobalmargi. One hour to position the parties and at the latest, we should be hitting them by 0600 hours. We'll take two troops under Ash and myself. Bobby, you stay back, you went for the last operation, but keep a couple of guys ready in case they are required.'

'That's unfair sir,' said Bobby, in a tone that Harry knew, meant he was going to argue. 'Just when you have confirmed intelligence and I know there's going to be a contact, you drop me out. I am in, now where you insert me is what you have to decide.'

Harry knew it was pointless arguing with Bobby in such situations. In fact, he quite liked the spirit and would have been surprised had he not forced himself into the operation.

'I suggest,' said Harry, 'you drop us off at Z Gali and come back in the vehicles till Gagal. The vehicles can go back to the post and you could, with your party, position yourself slightly above the village at the edge of the jungle at Andarnar. That seals off one direction of escape, if the militants run down. The other side remains open, and we don't have enough troops to plug that exit. Too bad, the lucky ones can live a little longer. After all *Jehad-e-Kashmir* is here to stay for a long time to come.'

The incessant rain had ceased its constant patter and the only sound was of the nala, which was a raging torrent now, as rainwater furiously fought its way to the main river below. Patches of ominous rainclouds pockmarked the sky, waiting for a wind to unite them. Dim stars flickered in the muted moonlight. A falling star stitched a silver path across the firmament, disintegrating behind a patch of clouds. Unlike the Gujjar guides, the Indians considered it a lucky omen. Harry wished a silent success to the operation. The grey road stretched languorously through villages and fields to disappear where it snaked its way up, towards the pass at Z Gali. Driving without headlights, the potholes invisible with water, it was a test for both man and machine. Harry saw the frown of concentration on the young driver's face, the wince of pain at subjecting his machine to the punishment every time the vehicle landed in a pothole and groaned. He felt his innards rattle, like a dice before a throw. The road had turned into an obstacle course to hell.

A quick hurried handshake in the darkness, the clang of rifles being cocked, the click of the safety catches, whispered last instructions and the raiding party was negotiating its way along a treacherous track, which even a mountain goat would have steered clear of, even on a pleasant summer day. The path followed the razor sharp, thin, rocky spur, which came down from the Khobalmargi top. Harry got the impression that the path might just follow the spur right to the top, making it a comfortable easy trudge.

Behind, the lights of the Army post at Z Gali were visible and the dull throbbing sound of the generator carried to the men, a reassurance of the civilisation they had left behind. The vision of the sparkling lights on the dark hillside spoke of comfort and most wished they were back in camp. They were a group and yet each man was alone, carrying his weight and his thoughts. Bloody staff officers, thought Harry, probably sitting around the *bukhari*, with their drinks, watching TV and cursing the army. He saw the lights and realised how vulnerable to attack, the post was. If he had been a mujahidin, he would definitely have let off a few rockets at the post.

Below, on his left, he saw the faint flicker of lamp light on the vast black swathe of the mountain—probably the light of Doban village, or maybe a shepherd's hut. In the brief flashes of lightning, one saw a struggling mass of figures. An odd curse or the clang of metal on rock would punctuate the silence, as someone would slip. Then, at a hanging nala, the track left the top and dropped down. Very soon, the reassuring lights of the post disappeared as they went deeper into the folds of the mountain. The going was easy now, but each man knew from experience that if there was a downhill, a climb was always round the corner and the climb started suddenly.

The path came to an abrupt end at the base of a huge cliff, split in the middle. Harry put his head down, shifting the straps of his pack to ease the pain in his shoulders and followed the man in front, up through the gap in the rocks. It was more a goat trail than a track, and the men had to be pulled up by those ahead. It was a backbreaking three hours before they emerged out of the rocks and onto a well-used, grassy path. They hit the top just as the day was beginning to break. The weather had cleared and it promised to be a beautiful day. Harry called for a brief halt and the men sprawled down on the track, leaning against the rucksacks. The experienced hands who knew the uncertainties of combat, immediately pulled out their breakfast and began munching, regaining lost energy.

Harry took a sip of water and looked across the expanse. From his position, Z Gali was across the valley below him and he could make out the tiny white huts and the tents of the post. He saw the road, visible in places through the forest, like a serpent coiling its way up from Kalaruch to Z Gali. Then his attention was caught by a range of snow-clad mountains, in the far distance. A string of fluffy white clouds lazily drifted across the breadth of the range, covering the lower part of the mountains. Just above the clouds, he thought he saw the pinnacle of a peak towering head and shoulders, above its neighbours. Harry wondered about the range.

He pulled the map over his lap and ran an eye across the sheet, as he chewed on a dry puri. The Gujjar guide spoke up, as if reading his thoughts.

'That's Gilgit, *jenab* and the white mountain that you see, is Nanga Parbat.'

The major looked at the savage shape of Nanga Parbat, rising eight thousand metres and clearly visible now in the rising sun. Technically one of the most difficult mountains to climb and if looks were to be the judge, it lived up to its formidable reputation. The sight excited the mountaineer in him. As he watched, he wondered at the fundamentalist adventurers that these jehadis, who came from the land of the big mountain, were. The sight aroused in him, romantic feelings of exploration. He wished he had been born a hundred years back, where it would have been possible for him to trek across to the Northwest frontier.

'You have been there?' he asked the Gujjar, pointing to the mountain.

'Yes, *jenab*, briefly on my way to Kabul. We had taken a few days off and visited both Gilgit and Hunza, but in beauty nothing can beat our side of Kashmir.'

'And what about the women, Kadir?' Harry asked smiling.

'Ours are better any day, *jenab*, but we had a lot of fun in Peshawar. Good women and very cheap.'

Ash walked up the track, sharing a word with the men as he passed them.

'Time to part sir, we are already running late and I have a gut feeling there is going to be a contact.'

'Right, Ash. Take care, and remember, no unnecessary bravado! Good hunting.'

Sher Khan looked up at the water dripping through the green plastic sheet that had been spread between two rocks to make a shelter. He shifted his sleeping bag into a dry corner and surveyed his surroundings. The hideout was split by a thin nala, which came straight down from the Khobalmargi top. A few men were sheltering under the overhanging rocks across the nala, about fifteen metres away. There was a small area for cooking and another for rations and stores. The hideout could accommodate seven to eight people; there were ten today, and two of them were busy stringing up a bivouac now, between a clump of trees. Other than Sher Khan, Gul and Sheshwar, there were two other foreign militants. The rest were local Kashmiri boys from the villages in Lolab. Malik was absent; he had gone with Tiger, one of the battalion commanders, to Dardpura in south Lolab.

The hideout looked over a narrow valley, where a couple of nalas disgorged their content into the main stream. Behind, the mountain rose to a height of nearly three thousand metres, at an eighty-degree gradient. The jungle was dense, with huge deodar trees jostling for space, and thick undergrowth eating up the gaps in between. One couldn't see beyond ten metres into the jungle. In spite of the heavy rain, it was not difficult to stay dry. Very little rain escaped through the thick green canopy above. Sher Khan was satisfied with the selection of the hideout. It had enough cover.

As a habit borne out of experience and training, he went out and mentally ran through the various emergency situations—the different directions of attack, if the army carried out a raid and the possible escape routes. They couldn't be hit from behind since the gradient was too much, he thought. If the army came, which was doubtful in this weather, they would probably follow the main stream uphill, provided they had a guide who knew where the camp was. Improbable, since it was a new camp and they hadn't had any militants who may have had an idea of the camp's location, surrendering. In any case, the Army was definitely not going to climb three thousand-metres in the rain. Any informer would guide the army up from Gagal village, which was about an hour's walk downhill from the camp, reasoned Sher Khan. An attempt from that direction and they would make such a racket through the undergrowth, he thought, they may as well come beating the drums.

'That man,' said Sher Khan to one of the local militants who was busy stirring a pot over a stove. 'The one who carried our rations—is he reliable?'

'Nothing to worry, *jenab,*' answered the man. 'He cannot leave his cattle and in any case he is mad and nobody would believe him. You know, he speaks to his cattle and complains of head problems. Nobody comes into this part of the Kafiristan jungle. The army doesn't. They don't know about the place. The villagers can't bring them either, for none of them have been allowed in here for grazing or cutting wood, in years. You are as safe here, as a child in the mother's womb.'

'Agreed,' said Sher Khan, checking his watch. 'A bit wet and uncomfortable, but a good selection nevertheless. Very secluded and secure. Time to make the evening report to Mike Charlie (MC) in Pakistan and check with Malik about how things are at his end,' he said, getting up.

'How far to the hide?' asked Ash. 'We are already late. We should have hit it by six and it's nearly eight now. Everybody is going to be up and about in the hideout by now.'

'Another ten minutes, *jenab,*' whispered Alia. 'I told you to take the route up from the village, but major sahib insisted that he would approach the camp from behind. Look at the angle of the ground. You have to dig your heels in to stop from rolling down. This takes time.'

Ash looked around and made eye contact with the man to his right. The tension was noticeable on his face. Ten men in a horizontal line were slowly making their way down. It was painstaking work. Every step was measured and the ground they trod on, was checked for any broken twig, or loose earth. The gradient was too steep and they had to dig a tiny step with their heels before placing their feet. Ash realised he had never been so alert, so focused in his life. His senses blended, making him one with Nature.

Even the omnipresent sound of the river, common in the Lolab Valley, was absent in this part of the jungle, making the silence conspicuous enough to be loud. He could hear his heart beating like a piston against his ribcage. He was worried his heart might get damaged. This is the worst part, he thought. The uncertain wait. You die a hundred deaths waiting for the real thing. Let the fireworks start and he would be all right.

The jungle was thick and foreboding and the early morning sun preferred to flirt with the treetops. Mist swirled around the trees creating an eerie setting in an already tense atmosphere. Visibility was poor, and Ash was worried they might walk into the hideout before realising they had hit it. He looked up and saw a fluffy brown owl looking at him, as only an owl can. Was he trying to tell him something; the presence of danger or the possibility of death? He banished the thought immediately. It was just an owl, and it couldn't even see in the daylight. He gave a quick glance on either side to ensure that everybody was in visual contact and advancing together. The smell of damp earth and rotting vegetation was overwhelming and the sudden, foul smell of human excreta was sharp and pungent. He turned and saw the soldier on the periphery point toward a cluster of rocks, then run a finger across his throat, his expression a mixture of worried alarm and excitement.

Poor camp discipline, my boys. This is going to be one expensive shit, thought Ash as he tiptoed across to the soldier, his eyes travelling in the direction indicated. A head was bobbing up and down in the nala. The militant was probably washing his face. They had hit the hideout. Like a child in a toyshop, for seconds, Ash just sat there confused, gathering his thoughts. He didn't know the layout of the hideout. Should he go down further or open fire now? Where were the rest of the militants? God, he thought, you give me surprise and confuse the situation. Why couldn't you have had them sitting in a row, offering namaz?

He tapped the pressure switch of his radio thrice, and hoped Harry or somebody in his party would receive the pre-arranged signal they had sighted the camp and were about to engage. He made an approximate guess to the layout of the hideout, and indicated with his arm for the line to swing in towards the nala. He checked his safety catch, adjusted his bullet-proof *patka*[1], breathed the name of the god he worshipped and then went down, towards the only militant he had in sight. A bird in the nala, he thought is better than two in an unknown bush.

Ash opened the account, with two shots into the militant in the nala. The man hit the rock with his face, and then crumpled into the thin stream. Liquid met liquid and the water turned a murky red. The jungle reverberated with the sound of gunfire, as the skirmish became individualistic in nature. Ash stood on top of the main camp, blazing away at some movement in the bushes to the right. The mujahidin were on the run and in the heat of action, all drills were forgotten, as adrenaline clouded the brain. The next instant, he had crashed through the plastic sheets of the hideout to land on a sack of rice. The bullet fired from maximum range entered through his stomach and hit his spine. With no power to break the spine and escape, it turned upward and zipped inside him, like a fly in a bottle looking for an opening and damaging his vital organs beyond repair. Ash was barely conscious when his men found him.

Sher Khan, Gul and a local militant had just stepped out of the hideout and were four hundred metres below on their way to the village, when the first shots rang out. He looked up towards the hideout and briefly, thought that he should go back and fight.

'*Jenab*!' he heard the local militant shout in alarm. 'Run! The army has raided the camp!' With that, the man turned and disappeared

[1] Half helmet used by the soldiers in Indian army.

into the undergrowth and was devoured instantly by the voracious mist creeping up the valley and saving him for another day of madness.

Sher Khan stood there in shock. He couldn't believe that the army had come down that route and in the worst possible weather. Briefly, the mist parted and he had a glimpse of a soldier standing on the rocks above the hideout blazing away, quite oblivious to the danger around, as if he were casting a line on a peaceful day. It infuriated Sher Khan to see the soldier with utter disdain, calmly firing away, while the mujahidin scattered around like rats. Nothing could be more insulting, he thought. The distance was great and out of sheer frustration he took aim and fired a single shot.

Sher Khan had the brief satisfaction of seeing the man topple over, as the bushes around him crackled to gunfire. He saw the mountainside across suddenly come alive to the hollow bark of assault rifles. Strangely, the ping sound of gunfire now reminded him of his childhood in Muzzafarabad, where after school, a hundred kids would run sticks along an iron railing that enclosed the cemetery, on their way home. He had no time to think, as his legs carried him along the easiest path, downhill towards the village, which his befuddled mind told him, should be the last place of refuge.

An Encounter

She walks in beauty, like the night
Of cloudless climes and starry skies;
And all that's best of dark and bright
Meet in her aspect and her eyes.

—Lord Byron

HARRY AND HIS party had used one of the spurs, running down from the Khobalmargi top, and were now in ambush across the main stream in the valley, between the hideout and the village. He had received Ash's radio signals alerting him and a little later heard the fire fight raging in the jungle. He stood up at the sound of gunfire and scanned the jungle in the hope of seeing the action. But it was too thick. He tried to figure out from the sound of the gunfire, whether Ash was receiving any incoming fire, but that again was difficult to make out, as both parties carried the same weapons.

Harry saw the bushes below and across the stream moving, as a large body came crashing through, heading towards the stream. Hold fire, he told himself, they will cross the river and climb straight up in his direction. Then a single shot was heard from below, and all hell broke loose, as his men opened up in the general direction of the shot. The movement in the bushes gained urgency and changing direction, it swung away from them, towards the village further downstream.

Without a second thought, Harry was rushing down headlong through the undergrowth. He waded through the stream, hit an unused track, overgrown with bushes, and ran as if all the spirits of all the mujahidin killed in the Jehad were after him. He emerged out of the jungle, hit a flat field and a hundred metres ahead, saw a house. He slowed, taking in the lay of the ground. Searching villages was always a nightmare, a dicey job even in the best of times, he thought. From a first floor side window of the house, he saw a man jump into a vegetable patch, weapon flying out of his hands at the impact of the fall.

Harry, his chest heaving with exertion, knelt and fired two rounds in succession at the figure. The man turned and looked at him straight, and their eyes locked briefly, over fifty metres of hatred. Harry had missed. He cursed loudly and his fingers curled around the trigger. Before he could fire, a woman rushed out of the house and stood in the line of fire. Harry hesitated. Only the militant's head was visible, towering over the woman. It was a difficult shot under any circumstances. The radio strapped to his chest crackled and a worried voice came on the air calling for him.

'Two-Zero, Two-Zero, if you hear me. Two-Two, is hit. I say again, Tiger hit, Over.'

Harry knew Ash was wounded. He heard someone from behind shout.

'*Maro* sahib, *maro*[1]. Take the shot, what are you waiting for!'

Everything went into slow motion for Harry. His breathing had levelled out and his head was clear. He could hear the gurgling

[1] Shoot him sir, shoot him.

sound of a small stream close by, the radio transmitting its ominous commentary, as someone tried to pacify the excited operator and make sense how bad Ash's condition was. He could hear the soldier behind shouting in desperation and then literally pleading with him to engage and shoot the woman, if required. There was a strange out-of-body experience, an unusual calm, as if he was watching himself in an outdoor theatre and the plot was already known to him. Harry took a deep breath and lowered his weapon.

Sher Khan turned and gave him a lingering look. Harry saw the long hair, the black shalwar kameez, camouflage jacket, the hunted look in the militant's eyes. Then with a toss of his long hair, Sher Khan bounded into the eight-feet high maize crop bordering the house. The soldier behind, in desperation, emptied his magazine in the general direction Sher Khan had taken. But Harry knew it was a futile gesture. The mujahid would live to fight another day.

Harry slowly walked up to the house, listening to the babble of excited conversation on the net.

'Cover the girl and get everybody out of the house. I want to have a word with them,' he told the soldier with him, who was busy inspecting the maize field, hoping a lucky shot may have got his quarry. 'Two-Zero for all stations, stay on listening. Two-Two, report over,' he spoke tersely into the radio.

'Six kills, Two-Zero. Ash sahib wounded; have given him first aid and he is on his way down. I am searching the camp with ten men. Over.' Harry realised the man had his emotion under control now. The combat effect was wearing out. He too was feeling absolutely drained and drowsy and there was a peculiar lightness of mind and body. It would be a most satisfying experience, he thought, to sleep under the shade of a tree, with the gentle gurgle of the stream to wash away the fatigue and madness of the last few hours. It was the extreme contrast of changes, emotional, physical and psychological, in the body, happening within minutes, that reduced one to such a state. The hours of mental build up, to be released in a few minutes of high-risk excitement, created that pure exhilaration of survival and made combat incredibly memorable, and exciting, even more so than sex.

'Two-Two, quickly take Ash down to Bobby sahib's party,' Harry continued speaking on the radio. 'He will organise the evacuation. I am sending some villagers to help carry the dead militants down. Roll up fast, and join me, while I spend some time searching the village. You heard that Bobby. Acknowledge. Over.'

'Wilco Two-Zero,' came Bobby's crisp voice. 'Will keep you informed on Ash. Good hunting.'

'Right,' said Harry, addressing the occupants of the house. 'What is the connection and how are you involved with militancy?'

The two of them exchanged looks. The old man and the daughter who had covered Sher Khan.

'I have no idea what you are talking about,' replied the old man. 'I was in the house the whole time, while the firing was happening. I am a poor Gujjar and because my house is at the periphery of the jungle, militants do come here from time to time for food. You come with a gun, I'll give you what you want. What choice do I have *jenab*?'

'This girl helped a militant escape,' said Harry, looking at the girl, who was trying to avoid his eyes, 'I spared her life. Now out with the truth. Why did you cover him? You are having an affair with the man, aren't you? Which means the whole lot of you are involved? What's your name, girl?'

'Sahira, *jenab*,' she said. '*Allah-talla* knows, I have never seen that man before in my life. Yes I did shield him, only because I didn't want any bloodshed on my doorstep and run the risk of our house getting destroyed. I would have done the same for you, *jenab*.'

'Bloodshed at your doorstep, when the entire valley is bloody!' interjected Harry in exasperation.

He sized her up. Physically she was short like most of her kinsmen, but extremely beautiful, and that too amongst a race where given the opportunity, every second woman could have graced the cover of fashion magazines. She was dark by the standards of her people and maybe that was what set her apart. She had a sharp small nose, with black, blazing eyes. Eyes which would haunt a man, long after he had left the presence of the woman. Her hair was the colour of her eyes, and fell much below her waist in thick waves. She must have been in her early twenties and still retained an air of innocence quite rare amongst women her age and community. Most were married and became mothers very early. Coupled with hard living and responsibilities, beauty and youth were fleeting. But it was her carefree, fearless spirit which would have drawn men to her in any part of the world.

Even now, she was facing Harry with no sign of nervousness or fear and confessing all the time that she had helped the mujahid to escape at great personal risk and that she would do it for any man under the same circumstances. The strange thing was, Harry realised, he believed every word Sahira spoke. Was it the long absence of women in his life, Harry wondered, that made him so vulnerable to females? Or was it the long period of exposure in similar insurgency situations that had made him soft to such often repeated theatrics; theatrics witnessed in different places, by different people, in different languages, across the length and breadth of the country. He turned to the father.

'If there has been so much militant movement recently, don't you think it was your duty to report the intelligence to the army, or is it your tacit way of helping the movement?'

'*Jenab*, I don't give your information to them,' answered the father, 'and neither do I pass their information to the army. We just want to be left alone. We are on no one's side.'

'That's why Allah is punishing you,' replied Harry, raising his voice and getting agitated at the old man's attitude. 'You have got to take a side, old man, otherwise you are contributing to the longevity of this misery, and living in a fool's paradise. You don't start and solve issues like this by staying neutral and waiting to drift to the winning side. Tell me, why did you start this jehad nonsense in the first place? I can understand Srinagar or Baramulla, but what was the necessity for you people in Lolab to pitch in? How many times before this madness erupted, has the so-called Hindu army come here and troubled you? Come on old man, give me a reason! You have to take a side and I am trying to help you to take a decision. Next time I come here, I must know where you stand, and if I find you still sitting on the fence, I'll assume you are with the mujahidin. Allah protect you from my wrath then.'

'*Jenab*, there was a time when the devil's wind blew from Srinagar to Muzzafarabad and Lolab was caught in the middle. Independence was in the air and every man and his boy went across to Pakistan to get themselves the magic wand, the AK rifle. You know how it is, *jenab*. If I don't have a weapon and my neighbour has one or his son does, he is in a better bargaining position in life. The weapon becomes the equaliser. And then poverty and unemployment compound the problem.

'Jehad has nothing to do with the Kashmiri youth taking up arms. Some did for that reason, but the majority didn't. Now all that has cooled off and we are paying a price for our mistake.

My daughter here is a widow. Her young husband was killed in inter-group violence. Barring a few local militants, who with the help of the guest mujahids, do mischief to the security forces, the majority are just surviving and waiting for better times. They can't surrender for fear, that the army would move out some day, and then they and their families would be easy targets for the foreign militants.'

'As if those better times will come with more people like you around,' replied Harry, his anger cooling down now. 'And what independence do you want, or do you actually believe Pakistan will give you more of it? If you are talking about poverty, come and see my part of the country, and you'll come back thanking Allah for his generosity. I have never seen a Kashmiri without shoes, or without a few fruit trees to his name, or for that matter, minus a roof over his head. Go along the Kalaruch road, and you will come across Bihari road labourers, living in leaking, miserable makeshift huts, made out of tar drums. They have no permanent house, no land they can call their own, and no homeland to go back to. They live and die on the road. That is poverty.'

'It's not a question of who will give more independence,' answered the old man. 'We didn't want to be with anybody. But views have changed. The *aawam*[2] realises the Pakistani game plan, and things are not any better across the border. But *jenab*, the die is cast, and it's not in your hands or mine, to stop destiny.'

'Yeah! Sure,' said Harry. 'The perfect impotent attitude to keep all sides happy. But it's in my hand to shoot those that are trying to play with destiny. I am a professional soldier and take great pride in that. It doesn't matter in the end which way Kashmir goes, but while I am here, who cares who wins, my job is to fight, so keep

---

[2] Populace

that in mind and pass the message along to your friends in the mountains.'

Harry picked up his weapon, looked at the girl who held his gaze with a mischievous twinkle in her dark eyes, as if she had tested and seen through Harry's tough exterior and knew that beneath the dark, brooding exterior, there was a good heart ticking. The smouldering look would remain and summon him again to her presence, he was certain of that. And he was sure the tall mujahid she had helped escape would follow suit, a victim to her charms, like him.

'*Khuda hafiz*[3], we shall meet again,' he said. Then indicating to the men to follow, Harry went down through the maize field, onto the track, that skirted the village of Gagal.

---

[3] May God be your guardian, a term used while taking leave of some one

Maktub

IT IS WRITTEN (ARABIC)

(1340 HRS)

How can man die better, than facing fearful odds,
The ashes of his father, the temples of his God.
—Indian Army Memorial, Razangla Pass

On the way back, Harry's thoughts turned to Ash and he called for the radio operator to get Bobby on the set. He leaned on his rifle and admired the view, waiting for the operator to patch up. It was nearly mid afternoon and the bright sun was rapidly absorbing the sogginess of the valley, leaving everything fresh and clean. The houses looked washed, their tin roofs shimmering; the mountains wore a greener look. The stream, rid of the night's mud, was so clear that sunlight reflected off the silver barbs darting up to the surface. The lower slopes were carpeted with a profusion of wild flowers of different varieties in a burst of vivid colours. Harry plucked a daisy and shoved it into the lapel of his battle dress.

'This flower, back in Delhi,' he told the operator behind him, 'costs five rupees.'

'Really, sahib?' said the man showing polite interest and plucking one.

Harry noticed the rest of the men following the officer and collecting flowers, shoving them in their rifle barrels and battle dress. He realised that there was something soft and gentle about flowers that had touched the men, especially after the rough, violent twenty-four hours that they had gone through. He curbed the urge to check them from doing such an un-soldierly thing; plucking flowers and using their barrels as a vase. If they had a contact now, he thought, they would be firing flowers at the mujahidin. What a bunch of sissies they would look, to any militant watching them through binoculars. The men were in high spirits and Harry didn't want to spoil the mood. Anything over five kills was a good bag. The operator said something and then passed the hand set to Harry.

'Two-Zero, over,' Bobby's voice came across loud and clear from Kupwara.

'Pass, over,' said Harry.

'Bad news, boss,' there was a brief pause, in which Bobby's breathing was audible, 'Ash is dead.'

Harry slumped down, and within seconds the bad news had spread down the column to the last man. No words needed to be spoken; the officer's body language was good enough for the men to fathom that something terrible had happened. The inane banter died as each man withdrew into himself, thinking of the dead man. Ash had been a good officer, a fine man, and popular with the others. The loss would affect them. Harry thought of Ash's parents and his young sister. Ash had often talked about his concern to settle her. He had always wanted her to pursue her studies and go abroad.

Well, thought Harry, his parents wanted to see their son in uniform and they had at least had the satisfaction of seeing him, although briefly. I must write a letter to them and pay them a visit in Nagpur if possible. It suddenly struck him that Ash may have had a girl somewhere who might need to be informed. Probably not, he reasoned immediately. Ash never mentioned anything about a girl. Where was the bloody time? A military school somewhere in the back of beyond, to the National Defence Academy for three years, to the Military Academy for a year and finally commissioned into the infantry and straight to an operational area. Where was the bloody time and opportunity to woo women? It suddenly struck him that Ash probably died a virgin. The militants were better off in this regard, he realised—at least they had a woman whenever they wanted.

Harry wanted to delay hitting the post; it would rake up memories. He looked across at the paddy fields, as a gentle breeze swept the valley, sending a ripple across the paddy crop, as if a giant unseen hand was passing over it. Harry imagined it to be Ash's soul, passing over the valley for the last time, on its way to his gods in heaven. He heard the sad song the women were singing, while they planted the rice sapling. Such a beautiful valley, he thought, and so much unhappiness.

'What are they singing about?' he asked the Kashmiri guide with him. 'If they are singing about me and making fun of me, I will fire a burst over their heads!' Harry was aware how these songs were created, in the spur of the moment, and he had been a subject before, for one of these planting and singing sessions.

'It's a sad song, *jenab*,' said the guide. 'It has nothing to do with you, but definitely with the army. They're singing of some old incident, maybe it happened here or in some other part of the valley.'

'Well translate it for me,' said Harry. 'I like the tune. It has the right note of melancholy.'

'*jenab*, the song is called the *Grave under the Chinar Tree* and this is how it roughly runs:

She stood by the stream, a veil over her face,
Wearing a white phiran[1], *an exquisite work of lace.*
Safina Lone was from the village Meen,
She waited for her lover,
an area commander of the Hijbul-Mujahidin.

He would come on Fridays, knowing she had that evening free,
She would patiently wait for him, under the Chinar tree.
'If there be danger,' he had warned, 'well, wear something red,
I'll turn back at once, knowing there lurks a great threat'.

Thus these clandestine meetings, went on for a whole year,
When unknown to the two, the fauj[2] *heard about the bizarre affair.*
Sure enough on Friday, the village was cordoned off at three,
While the major and his buddy, climbed the Chinar tree.

Soon the army went back, leaving the villagers free,
Exactly at six, she was at her rendezvous, under the Chinar tree.
He stepped out of the jungle, looking at her white figure.
A quiet, nagging doubt, made him play with his rifle trigger.

He looked at the beautiful girl and his heart swelled with pride,
If I hadn't been a militant, he thought,
I could have made her my bride.
Javed, admiring her long tresses, and dreaming of her sensuous lips,
Walked on towards her, reaching halfway across the bridge.

The major steadying his rifle, suddenly knocked his cap,
Safina looking up shouted, 'Forgive me Javed,
for I have led you into a trap.'
The buddy fired fast, dropping Javed to the ground,

[1] A traditional gown worn by both men and women in Kashmir.
[2] Here, Indian army.

If the major hadn't stopped him,
he would have emptied his last round.

Safina ran forward, throwing herself on her dead lover,
Begging him to open his eyes, alas! Javed was gone forever.
The major stood at a distance, watching the pitiable sight.
A weeping woman, her dead lover,
and he wondered if what he had done was right.

The major walked up, to console the shattered girl.
'He had lived by the gun after all,' said he 'and had to die by one.'
Safina suddenly got up, her white phiran, blood red,
Picking up her dead lover's rifle, she shot the major dead.

Sepoy Surjeet Singh saw his sahib fall,
In a frenzy he fired, and Safina had joined Major Paul.
A pained expression creased his face, as he looked at the gory sight,
Fearing that his legs wouldn't hold him,
he held on to the railings tight.

He wept for his dead officer, a sahib with qualities great.
'You killed the snake, sahib, you shouldn't have spared its mate.'
The blood dripping from the bodies, turned the brook red,
Spreading the tragic tale to the villages far ahead.

Those who came and saw, realised the futility of war,
You will still hear it talked about, in Kashmiri lore.
The major was taken away and buried with full military rites,
Mourned by a young woman who'd spend many a lonely night.

The other two have all the time, for they are finally free.
They lie buried together, under the Chinar tree.
And if you ask us, we'll tell you of moonlit nights;
You'll find them crossing the bridge hazoor,
heading towards the Putshai heights.'

Shumrial Village (Lolab)
(0800 HRS)

Faire et se taire.
'Shut up and get on with it.'
—Gustave Flaubert

JAVED JABBAR FROM the corner of his eye watched Sher Khan pace up and down, ranting all the while about the non-cooperation of the Kashmiris. He measured the small room with his long strides, his chin sunk on his chest, his long hair falling over his face from either side, hiding the grief in his eyes from the others sitting around quietly.

'Sheshwar *shaheed*, just because there was an informer, who should have been dealt with by your people,' said Sher Khan, looking at Javed sharply.

'Relax, *jenab*,' said Javed. 'Why keep talking about Sheshwar? Four Kashmiri mujahidin also died with him. We'll try and find the culprit.'

Sher Khan gave him a sharp look, his dislike for Javed quite noticeable.

'It's the man who carried our rations,' said Sher Khan. 'He is the only man who could have guessed the location of the hideout. I am going to pay him a visit now.'

'*Mohtram,*' said Javed, addressing Sher Khan in a respectful manner, quite aware of his feelings towards him. 'That man is sick and mad, and the only company he keeps is of the cattle. I have known him for years. Leave him alone, we'll find the informer.'

'We'll see. Now shut up and get on with it' said Sher Khan picking up his weapon and calling for Gul to follow.

Harry blew out the flame of the incense sticks, before it threatened to turn into a mini fire, with his hand, and watched the thin, grey smoke spiral energetically upward. He waved a hand through the smoke, and a strong odour of jasmine jarred his senses. Too strong, he thought. He closed his eyes and prayed to Sai Baba, requesting the one thing any combat leader in command of men wishes every time he prays—let no man die under my command. He opened his eyes and his gaze fell on Ash's photograph, now pinned in one corner of the map, hanging on the wall in his room. His attention shifted to the other corner immediately, where a photograph of the man who had killed him, had been pinned as well.

They had found a camera with a half-used roll in the hideout, which had promptly been developed at Kupwara. Most of the snaps were of military garrisons, in and around Lolab, while a few had mujahidin posing for the camera in some jungle hideout. A tall man in black shalwar kameez, with long hair and cradling an AK rifle with a grenade launcher attached, had caught Harry's attention. He had recognised the face instantly as that of the man who had been saved by the girl. The weapon in the picture was with them, picked up from where it had been left, by the fleeing mujahid.

Harry had put two and two together and guessed that the man

in the snap was none other than Sher Khan. A pang of profound remorse had engulfed him at having allowed the man to live. He had gone over the entire scene a hundred times in his mind since, trying to justify his act, but had derived no comfort. For the life of one woman, he had saved another, who would snub out the life of so many others and had probably killed Ash, too.

He compared the two faces. One was a young man barely out of his teens, sporting a military crew cut, with an innocent half smile playing at the corners of his mouth and a face that radiated boyish energy. And the mature, hardened face of Sher Khan, that Harry remembered so well from their brief encounter, staring at the camera with the same intensity. The forehead was deeply creased and there were worry lines at the corner of the eyes. There was an attempt to smile, but the eyes remained absent of any humour. The face had the wild, caged look of someone brought up on a regular diet of hatred and vengeance, for whom happiness has been an occasional episode in the general drama of loss and violence. Reflexively, Harry picked up the hand mirror from the table and inspected his face.

A sensitive intelligent face stared back at him. He was born fair, but too many years of the sun and wind had taken its toll on the exposed skin, turning it dark brown—the colour of a walnut. except for the sprinkling of grey noticeable in his hair, and the odd laugh lines under his eyes, the face looked younger than its thirty-three years. To a perceptive looker, the maturity far beyond his age was noticeable in his eyes; eyes which had lost the exuberance of its youth in the volatile war in Sri Lanka. Women had often commented on those eyes, saying that they carried a lot of melancholy and sensitivity, hidden otherwise in the general façade of the happy-go-lucky attitude that he projected. They had also found him attractive, with a terrific sense of humour.

He had grown up all over the country, following his father who was a colonel in the Paras. His father cultivated in him the qualities of fair play. Honour of the family and the gentleman's code of conduct—fight fair and fight hard and let the best man win. Standing six feet in his socks, Harry had excelled at boxing in the Military Academy, earning a blue in the sport and had later taken up distance running and climbing. He had gone on a few army and regimental expeditions and before being posted in the valley, had scaled Nanda Devi at the cost of a couple of toes lost to frost bite. It was a small loss compared to one's life, for the weather at seven thousand metres had turned nasty and Harry and his climbing buddy had lost the fixed rope on the way down. They had been forced to bivouac for the night. The next morning his buddy was in no shape to move and Harry, in spite of his own deteriorating condition, had managed to bring him down nearly four hundred and sixty metres before running into the rescue party. He was awarded a Sena Medal for bravery by the army. The experience had only fuelled his passion for climbing and the outdoor life.

Harry kept the mirror back and shifted his attention back to Ash's photograph. He realised that he would have to pay a visit to Ash's parents. His sister was to be married in winter. The parents would probably delay it now. God, he thought. Thirty-three, and I take the name of God more than a sixty year old in Delhi does.

'The men are ready for your debriefing, sahib,' said the senior *subedar*, who had probably been standing at the door respectfully, waiting for him to break out of his reverie.

Bobby bought the men to attention as Harry walked out.

'All in, sir,' he said saluting, 'except for the ration collection party.'

Harry ran a quick look over the assembly. The old, seasoned, battle-scarred *subedar*s and havildar sat behind on wooden benches, their impassive weather beaten faces difficult to read. In their nearly two decade of service they had seen it all, from Sri Lanka to Kashmir and there were few surprises that combat could spring now, to shake them. The pillars who had always held the Indian army, passing the traditions and values from generation to generation, thought Harry. The younger lot sat on a tarpaulin spread on the ground, the shadow of grief visible on their sun burnt young faces, as they looked up eagerly at the company commander, in anticipation of what he had to say. For most, it was their first taste of loss.

'Sit easy,' said Harry. 'To start with, let me say *shabash*.[1] Overall, a good operation. Good field craft, good fitness, good *josh*[2]. However, there are always things to be learnt from any operation. Now, who was detailed with Ash sahib as his buddy? Dilawar, I remember detailing you to keep a check on him. Where were you when he got shot?'

'Sahib, you know how he was,' replied Dilawar, his face worn down with lack of sleep and grief and well aware that all eyes in the company were on him now.

'We went down towards the hideout together and then all hell broke loose as firing started. The militants seemed to be more interested in escaping than putting up a pitched battle. I remember seeing him standing right next to me on the rocks firing, and the next instant he just rolled over. In fact, the firing had also subsided by then and I just don't know where the shot came from. All I can say sahib, is that his day had come.'

'I guess the bullet had his name written on it,' said Harry. 'Well, I think I saw the man who shot him. I wish I had known it then.

---

[1] Well done
[2] Enthusiasm

Let me confess,' he demurred, thinking about the right way to put it across, 'I stand guilty for letting off his murderer.' Briefly Harry tried to make eye contact with Havildar Saifullah Khan, the man who was behind him during the chase. The soldier averted his gaze. Harry was aware that the incident would be discussed in detail amongst the men. 'Well,' he continued, 'I had reasons for not engaging him. Some of you would not agree with my way of fighting this war. However, all I can say is, we will avenge Ash sahib's death, if that's the last thing we do, before parting from this valley of shadows. Now cheer up, we are in the profession of trading lives. Let Ash sahib's memory never fade. He was a good man and a fine officer.'

After the men had broken off, he summoned Alia, who had been sitting all this while on his haunches at the langar, with his head in his hands.

'You have done well,' said Harry, addressing him and affectionately patting his back. 'Bobby, make sure the guy gets a sack of rice and sugar and give him a hundred for his medicines. You take care Alia and the next time I visit you, give me tea with sugar. *Khuda hafiz*.'

Khobalmargi Meadow
(1800 HRS)

No formulae the texts book know,
Will turn the bullet from your coat,
Or ward the tulwars downward blow,
Strike hard who cares-shoot straight who can,
The odds are on the cheaper man.

—Rudyard Kipling

ALIA CHOPAN WAS trying to round up a very reluctant herd of cattle for the night, who like children were now trying to postpone the pleasures of grazing. Some pretended as though they hadn't heard his shrill whistles of command. Some were gradually trying to drift out of his line of sight, while others were munching the delicious grass at a furious pace, stuffing it into their mouths, to chew at leisure during the night.

Alia's whistle died on his lips as he saw the militants approaching. His migraine-battered brain told him he was in trouble.

'*Asalaam-walekum jenab*,' he greeted them, putting on his dumb expression, which had earned him the reputation of being retarded.

The men didn't answer. Alia recognised the three of them.

He knew Javed was a local and Alia was aware of his reputation for using the razor. He was more scared of Javed than the other two. The tall man with Javed confronted him, while the third man stood behind.

'Why did you do it brother?' asked the tall man. 'A *mukhbir*[1] of the kafirs, against your own brothers for a little money, a few bags of rice. How will you face Allah?'

Alia didn't answer. He couldn't. His tongue seemed to have got stuck to his palate. He swallowed hard trying to get his speech back, but he might as well have been dumb, his voice wouldn't come out. His Adam's apple bobbed up and down at a furious pace, giving the impression to Sher Khan that it might pop out of his mouth anytime, convincing him that the man was guilty. Sher Khan entered the log hut and there in the corner, saw a big sack of rice and other rations with the odd Indian army canteen markings. The evidence was enough for him to pass judgment.

Sher Khan looked deep into Alia's face for a long time, as if etching his face in his memory. Then having made up his mind, he exchanged a look with Gul. '*Zaba*,[2] he uttered under his breath, and looked down towards the valley. When he turned back, Gul was wiping the blade of his knife on the dead man's shirt, intonating the last words of a *kalma*[3].

Alia Chopan had finally got rid of his migraine. He lay on the ground, his small, emaciated figure crumpled like a battered doll, and his neck sliced like a watermelon from ear to ear. His cattle didn't have to play any more games with him. They were free like Alia Chopan's soul, in that desolate, unknown meadow.

---

[1] Informer
[2] Behead, execute
[3] Islamic prayer

'You didn't have to do that to a poor man, *jenab*,' said Javed, shocked at the extremity of the punishment.

Sher Khan gave him a long look.

'You won't produce anymore informers and your camps won't be raided in the future,' he answered, with a hard smile.

Javed was no novice to violence and he hadn't earned himself a reputation for savagery, for nothing. He had used the cutthroat razor on a few occasions in very much the same way that Gul had just used the knife. The razor gave a man a slower death. But the small, slain body of Alia touched a patriotic chord in his heart. This was his country, and this man was his kinsman. How could an outsider treat human life like that? Briefly, he thought of shooting the lot, controlling himself when he saw Sher Khan watching him closely.

'You hate me, don't you?' Sher Khan said, a smug, dry smile disappearing into his thick beard.

'The question of love or hate doesn't arise, *jenab*,' answered Javed. 'Those emotions were long severed when I decided to follow the path of jehad. Let's go, it's getting dark.' He turned abruptly and walked down the path, towards the village where the twinkling lamplights were sprouting in the gathering dusk, as villagers prepared for the night. Deep down in his heart, he knew that there would be a time and place to square this act, and *Insha' Allah*, he would.

Sher Khan watching from behind, knew he had made himself a dangerous enemy.

Gagal Village (North Lolab)

(1030 HRS)

Four things greater than all things are–
Women and horses and power and war.

—Rudyard Kipling

SHER KHAN SAT on a chair outside on the verandah, deep in thought, looking out towards the Kafirstan jungles. Sahira came out carrying a cup of *kahwa* and some pieces of roasted chicken. Over the past few months, she had come to know him better. She knew that he had a wife and child back home in Pakistan. She also had a woman's intuition of reading a man, and in Sher Khan, she saw a tired man, whose vanity wouldn't allow him to relax, because he was scared of facing the real world. This was all he knew and this is what he did best. She left him alone to his thoughts.

Sher Khan looked across to the mouth of the valley and tried to identify where their old camp had been. But the jungle canopy was too thick and the camp was tucked into the folds of one of the secondary nalas. He recalled his flight, that fateful day to Sahira's house. He vividly remembered the Indian officer's face and realised how close he had come to meeting his maker.

He wondered if he would have acquitted himself in a similar manner, if he had been in the other man's shoes. Probably not, he reasoned.

Over the months, he had taken a round of the valley and met the rank and file that was fighting the Jehad. He hadn't been very impressed. He realised there was a different motivation that drove the movement—money. He could see the comfortable pattern that insurgency had settled into, with all the main dramatis personae including the security forces, the villagers and the local playing roles to suit their comfort.

Most of the militants had picked their operational areas close to their villages. This gave them security, comforts of family and logistic support. Most collected a nominal fee from each house to augment their income, over and above the salary they received from their *Tanzim*. Sher Khan had tried to ban extortion from the locals, as it put the *aawam* against you. However, the local mujahids had insisted that as the funds from across were always late, they could not rely only on the salary. If militancy were to be sustained, then the locals would have to bear the burden.

This arrangement also made it difficult for them to engage in any sort of operation against the security forces, for fear of retaliation to their kith and kin by the latter. As a result, no operations were being conducted and false reports were regularly sent back to the controller in Pakistan. Sher Khan checked his watch, picked up his radio and got Malik on the air for the usual end-of-day situation report. They were in the midst of a conversation, when another station interrupted and a refined voice came on the air.

'*Asalaam-walekum*, Sher Khan,' said Harry. 'Care for a chat?'

'It's a *fauji* dog,' said Malik from the other end. 'Sheru bhai, switch channel two up.'

'Wait,' said Sher Khan. '*Haan fauji* bhai, what do you have to say?'

'Nothing important, just wanted to get your views on the progress of the Jehad. How close do you think *aazadi* is?'

'You and I are too small, *mohtram*, to set a time frame for such a huge event. That is in the hands of Allah. We are only his instruments. You see, your fathers and forefathers were used to slavery. Your generation seems to have forgotten that and what cannot be taught by words, we will teach at the point of a gun. We will see the land of Kashmir free, rid from the *zalim* rule of the Hindus.'

'Listening to you,' said Harry, 'I don't know if I should applaud you for your brave attempts, or laugh at your stupidity. I don't know which madrasa you went to and what history they taught there, but they really filled you up with this shit. I don't know if you realise that you are the cannon fodder for the Pakistani *hukumut*[1]. Their generals' and politicians' sons are not sacrificing their lives for this cause. But I guess if I had a few brainless, poor, social outcasts with me, I would also send them across to do my dirty work. You really think, Sher Khan that you can take on the might of a nation like ours?'

'Well, we did break the Russians and they were a super power. *Insha' Allah*, we shall see Hindustan scattered to the winds too. We are in no hurry and there is no dearth of volunteers flocking to our banner. We are used to all sorts of hardships and we bear it with fortitude, waiting for our death. As for brainless fools being pushed across, let me tell you I don't need to do this to earn a living and there are others with me who are landed people, *patwaris*[2], of their villages. Nobody pushed us. We came of our own free will and will leave Kashmir by our own free will. You sound like an officer, but I feel sorry for you *jenab,* sitting in your

[1] Government (Urdu)
[2] A village official who maintains land records.

bunker, fighting against your wishes and a member of a tired, scared army.'

'You can say that for the Paki army,' replied Harry, his voice conveying an undertone of anger. 'We have been in this game for many years now. This is just another job. As for being scared, where we come from, we don't hide behind petticoats. Next time you run into me, I may not be as generous.'

'Don't scare me with threats of death. I am no boy to this line of work. We had wrapped the shroud of death when we crossed into Kashmir and it would be a disappointment to leave alive. Incidentally, I didn't stand behind the woman—she covered me. Try and keep her out of this.'

'Well, if you are so desperate to die, Sher Khan, you and I could fix a place. Fight like a man. There are no heroics in using explosive devices or firing from across the valley.'

'You are losing your cool now, *fauji* bhai and you are sure to abuse. A mujahidin is forbidden to use bad language. So save your anger till we meet. *Fi Amanullah*.'

Anatomy of an Ambush
(2030 HRS)

For authentic living what is necessary,
Is the resolute confrontation of death.

—Martin Heidegger

THE WEATHER HAD turned chilly as winter approached. The land was shorn of all its resplendent colours and had taken on a dull, muddy hue. The walnut and poplar trees had shed their leaves and now stood naked, their branches stretched heavenwards, as if supplicating the weather gods to be kind. Ominous dark clouds gathered and dispersed. The sun became feeble, the streams fell silent, people wore a sullen look and even the incessant jabbering on the radio died down. There was an all-pervasive atmosphere of anticipation in the air. The cruel Lolab winter was knocking at the door.

'There is information sir,' said Bobby, 'that Sher Khan is regularly visiting that woman Sahira.'

'So I have heard,' answered Harry, who was busy writing a letter. 'We need to do a few more operations before the snow puts an end to all movement.' He put the pen down and turned around to face Bobby. 'Honestly at my age, it's quite an effort to force yourself to climb and spend the nights in the jungles,' he said.

'Come on, sir!' laughed Bobby. 'You are not that old. Early thirties is a man's prime and you still have a lot of physical work ahead of you. You aren't even married yet! And don't forget old Sher Khan, the cocky bastard on the radio…We still need to settle a score.'

'Settling that account is what keeps me going. Otherwise, by the standards of this part of the world and the speed of soldiering that I have done, a man withers fast. Look at the locals, especially the Gujjars. So good looking in their youth, and so quickly they age. How old do you think Salim is? You'll be surprised. He is just touching thirty and he looks and behaves like a fifty-year-old. It's all about the environment and the kind of life you lead. But I am surprised about this girl. I had warned her specifically not to get involved in this. Pity she was born in such trying circumstances.'

'Confess you have a soft corner for her sir,' Bobby said smiling. 'You are on your best behaviour in her presence. I think you have a crush on her too.'

'Yeah, what a waste of a good woman,' answered Harry. 'I wonder if she is aware of how beautiful she is. Anyway there is very little one can do about it. Our worlds are too different and the circumstances make the situation worse. Let's go pay her a surprise visit. Who knows, she might even present us with Sher Khan.'

The operation was planned for the following night. A party of thirty men under Harry and Bobby, climbed at night from a village called Surkuli, hitting Baran Gali before first light. The moon was in the second phase and the jungle looked creepy in the fading moonlight. Everything took on strange menacing shapes. Dead tree trunks looked like militants and the wind through the deodar trees often sounded like a whisper. The slightest noise made by the patrol, magnified many fold, and resounded so loud, that Harry was convinced it would alert some of the old timers in the village, who got up very early for the azan.

At a pond, which was a prearranged landmark, the party split into smaller, five men sub-units, to approach their respective ambush positions. It was still dark and the men settled behind bushes and trees, covering the track and overlooking the village below. Not a soul had stirred in the village. At the crack of dawn, the respective squad commanders came out of hiding and carried out the ambush correction drills. What in darkness may seem an ideal place for an ambush, especially when one is tired and looking for the first place to curl up in, may be a complete disaster in broad daylight. The old hands who had spent time in Sri Lanka, knew from experience of the numerous occasions when a party had been stalked and counter-ambushed by the Tamil Tigers, because of poor field craft.

The commanders walked down the track, wiping footprints in the designated killing area and sighting the automatics. They briefed the boys on the various landmarks and the deployment of the other neighbouring ambush parties. Fire orders were explained and various situations of contact that could arise were discussed in a whisper. Concealment was improved and then, each man donned his camouflage net, checked his weapon and settled down with his thoughts. While one man stayed on sentry duty, the majority preferred to doze. Before the first rays of the sun had made contact with the jungle floor, the party had become one with their surroundings. The toughest part of the anatomy of an ambush had begun—the wait.

Harry recalled reading somewhere, that one third of a soldier's life was spent in waiting. How true, he thought, of both peace and in war. All this effort and wait for twenty seconds of excitement.

He said a silent prayer for the success of the operation and the safety of the men. Then, like always, his imagination ran riot. He imagined Sher Khan walking down the track and getting shot. In his mind he could see the surprise on Sher Khan's face as he collected the first bullet and then, his body writhing on the ground. He improved on his fantasy and imagined capturing him alive.

Just imagining the various ways he would inflict pain to the guy, kept his mind occupied. Then his thoughts turned to Sahira. What if she was with him? He knew he would have to fire, even if it meant killing her. Deep down, he wished that she was not involved and that the information was incorrect. It surprised him that he was actually getting a hollow feeling in his stomach at the prospect of meeting her after the operation was over. They had to walk through the village, to where the vehicles would later pick them up. The track led past her house. He jerked himself back to reality and pulled out a book from his backpack. Leaning against his pack, he made himself comfortable, reading and dozing and wondering what other men his age would be doing in more civilised surroundings.

The ambush was well sited and it gave him the comfort of security. Harry recalled his early days in Sri Lanka as a rookie twenty-one year old lieutenant. He smiled as he remembered an ambush operation he had been tasked to carry out on an intelligence tip, that, the LTTE chief Prabhakaran's wife had been sighted washing her hair in a *kulum*[1]. The memory was vivid and he allowed his mind to drift down memory lane. Harry could see the faint Sri Lankan star light, the silhouette of the lead scout as he stopped and then, went down on his knees. The men behind, in the column, followed suit. An open field which may have been

---

[1] Pond (Tamil)

cleared for cultivation sometime in the past was now deserted and over grown with knee-high shrub and elephant grass. He remembered the feeling of vulnerability and nakedness in the absence of any cover. They were sitting ducks to any Tamil Tiger group if one of them was lurking in the area, at this time of the night. The safe, dark outline of the jungle in front beckoned.

'Lost, sahib,' whispered the lead scout. One of the most dreaded words for any combat commander. 'There should have been a pond here as per the map. We clearly took the wrong path at the last bound. Should we backtrack and get on to the other path?'

The other path was three hours behind, recalled Harry and that meant spending the whole night going up and down. He recalled the man's eyes in the darkness looking at him and waiting for a decision. Oh! How he hated these situations. Barely out of the military academy, he had volunteered and cleared the probation in a Special Force unit and had only recently been allowed to lead independent operations.

When you are inexperienced, young and entrusted with the command of leading a tough bunch of veteran fighters into combat, even the smallest decision magnifies manifold to become the mother of all problems—to go back or to continue? And if the latter, then where to? It was supposed to have been an ambush on a track coming out of the jungle that ran past the pond, to join up with the main Manar-Vavuniya road.

In desperation, he had led the column into some bushes and laid an ambush on an unused path, hoping he might run into some LTTE movement. At around two in the morning he had heard a great rumble in the jungle and had wondered if the LTTE were clearing the undergrowth with a road roller and coming after him. He had moved his men quickly to an abandoned hut, just in time, as a female elephant with a calf lumbered straight into the very same area where his men had taken up position! Harry remembered how they sat in mortal fear with weapons cocked for the next ten minutes as the mother picked up the smell of humans and went berserk, trumpeting, uprooting trees and trampling everything in her path. He recalled the conversation on the radio as he informed his company commander about the position getting compromised and untenable, because of elephants.

'Are you sure, Harry?' the major's faint, sleepy voice inquired, 'that these are wild elephants you are reporting and not LTTE trained?'

Well the tragedy of errors hadn't ended there for Harry. He took the patrol a few kilometres away to lay an ambush at a cross road leading into a village. The original mission had already been forgotten and the way to the golden pond where Prabhakaran's wife bathed was clearly guarded by angry elephants. The Indian army had still not worked out its operational response to this new weapon. He had, in all his young wisdom, selected a thicket of bushes overlooking the square where the four roads crossed each other rather close to the village, for it provided both cover for the team, surveillance of the village and a perfect killing ground.

Satisfied he had settled down, when at dawn, the first of the villagers had walked into the bushes where his men were concealed. He was promptly tied up and made to sit behind. Within the next half an hour another ten people had joined him—an old man, a young kid, a pregnant woman and having been rid of their fears of the army, were now animatedly chattering in Tamil. There was a small pond behind and Harry had realised that he had parked his ambush in the middle of the village shitting joint.

God, he thought as he opened his eyes. This place is a piece of cake compared to Sri Lanka.

At 1430 hours, the radio strapped to his chest buzzed and Bobby's excited voice came on the air.

'Two-One, Red Riding Hood coming out of the woods. Eleven o'clock to your position, you read, over.'

Harry crawled forward to a better vantage position and looked across, towards the track coming down from the Kafaristan jungles. He saw the lone figure of Sahira, carrying some utensils wrapped in a cloth, hurrying down towards her house.

'Roger that Two-Two, wait and watch, over,' replied Harry.

The distance couldn't have been more than three hundred metres across the stream and Harry could clearly see the expression on her face through the field glasses. She was wearing a red *phiran* and her black hair was tied in a bun with a piece of cloth. On her head she wore a Gujjar cap, with a cloth tail hanging down her neck. Harry knew she had gone up to meet someone in the jungle. The militants had banned all local movement in the area. Grazing and cutting wood was forbidden.

The jungle was thick here, with a lot of undergrowth and plenty of streams, which ran down various small nalas. The place was strategically located along the cross-country transit route, which ran in a north-south direction. Further, it had proximity to a village for logistic support and was difficult to cordon by the security forces, requiring a large body of men, which was not available. Unless one had an informer who had precise knowledge of the camp and was confident of taking you there, few army units would dare to enter the area for fear of buying unnecessary casualties. The terrain and the connectivity made getaways easy, in case of a raid by the security forces. The Kafiristan jungle had always remained popular as a sanctuary for temporary and permanent hideouts.

Harry watched as Sahira climbed the stairs to her house. She stood there briefly looking back towards the mountain she had come down and then disappeared inside. The men in the bushes waited for some new development, but a little later realised it may have been a false alarm when the curtains were finally drawn. A few hours passed without any activity. Excitement in the bushes subsided and the men soon became aware of the discomfort and the cold. Further down in the village, people could be seen going about their daily mundane chores. Some were working the fields, the women washing clothes in the stream and the kids playing, their laughter and screams faintly carrying up to the waiting men.

Sahira had spent the day with Sher Khan, in a temporary camp located barely half an hour's climb from her house, and just about three hundred yards from their previous camp, which had been destroyed by Harry some months back. In fact, some of the plastic sheets, utensils and the odd bit of crockery had been salvaged from the last camp. The sheets had been strung between trees and a small area underneath flattened, to accommodate sleeping. Nearby, a thin stream of fresh water trickled from under a rock, and provided for drinking, washing and cooking purposes.

The temporary camp had been established with minimum disturbance to the natural habitat and was in such harmony with its surroundings, that Sahira had actually stood there for sometime before she made out the two sheet bivouacs. The entrances were covered with deodar branches and all other items around were packed for a quick getaway and similarly camouflaged.

A sentry was posted during the day, at the edge of the forest line to keep an eye on the village below and the valley across. The camp was activated whenever Sher Khan was passing through or lying low, to get the security forces off his scent. One of his men would go down to Sahira's house to give her the information that

Sher Khan was around. It was only in the last two months that she had become physically intimate with him. He would drop in at the house off and on, always at night and leave early morning before the time of azan. Few words were exchanged and he would spend more time just watching her with dark, intense eyes. One look at him, and she could sense his heightened passion for her. With trembling hands he led her a little distance away from the other men in the camp.

In a secluded clearing under a huge fir tree they sat down and he asked her a few questions; how she was and had she been careful while coming here? He ran his fingers through her hair and slipped his hand through the top, to roughly fondle her breasts. He squeezed them to the point of pain as he pushed her down to the ground and savagely tugged at her shalwar strings. It scared her to see the intensity of his passion. It was animal-like in its nature. His eyes had a glazed look and his breathing was laboured. Men like Sher Khan did not know the meaning of gentle love making and the dominating, feudal nature was rather visible now, in this most basic of human needs. The given circumstances only enhanced these qualities.

In one quick move, he mounted her, plunging into her with a ferocity that shocked her. She could feel his weight on her, the thick beard brushing her face, as she closed her eyes, clenched her teeth and opened her legs further to accommodate him better. A few raging strokes, stifled moans and Sher Khan had expended his force. He lay spent, his head nuzzled in her neck breathing heavily. If he came fast, his recovery was even faster. The moment his heartbeat stabilised he was up on his feet, his senses alert to any danger. He averted meeting her gaze.

She got up slowly and assessed the damage. A couple of broken bangles, red marks on her arms that would probably bruise later and a tear in her kameez. She tied her hair and both of them walked back to camp. The two local Kashmiri militants ignored her, but she could feel their hostility towards her. The third was a foreigner—a thin, sparse man with alert eyes that kept darting back and forth. He had a gaunt face covered with a long matted beard. He gave her a bold gaze and went back to cleaning his weapon. Sher Khan opened the cloth bundle carrying the food and distributed the thick corn roti and sabzi she had cooked for them. Then she gave him a handful of walnuts. She quietly collected her utensils and looked at Sher Khan, who nodded his head for her to leave. He walked her down to the edge of the forest. She turned around to hug him, but saw that he had already distanced himself both physically and emotionally.

'I will drop in at your house in the evening,' said Sher Khan. 'Remember the signal; if there is no danger, you hang a red cloth on your balcony. *Khuda hafiz*,' and then he had stepped back into the shadows of the Kafirstan jungle, before she could return his farewell.

She had often thought of the major and waited for him. He had come across on a few occasions and had spent time sitting with them, discussing the future of Kashmir. She had offered him tea and dry walnuts and had requested him to stay for dinner. He looked tired and genuinely sad for the people of the valley. He often talked about the other parts of India and foreign travels and how people lived in safety and luxury. She loved listening to him. She couldn't understand what a sensitive, educated man like him could be doing in a violent profession like the army. Yet she knew that behind the sensitivity lay a streak of intense violence and determination.

It was only in the last few years, since the army had moved into Lolab had she seen men from the other parts of India. There were small, slit-eyed Gurkhas, who were very polite in their dealing with the locals, and there were hook-nosed, long-haired, bearded Sikhs who were very different from the Sikhs she had seen in Baramulla. She recalled taking a bus once with her friend, to go across to Rednag to see the dark men. Apparently they were from a Madras unit and came from way down south. Having met Harry she felt a little ashamed of having once joined a procession of women shouting slogans outside the District Collector's office in Kupwara for some custodial death. They had screamed their lungs out, threatening to go to Pakistan and come back with a baby.

From the furtive, shy looks Harry gave her, she was certain he found her attractive. During conversation, he looked at her often and tried to engage her in the general discussion. But behind the polite attempts, she could sense the restraint, as if he was conscious he was there for a job and any further encouragement to her was ethically incorrect. Or maybe in his culture, men and women intermingled freely and therefore the attempt on his part to encourage her to participate in the conversation. Her heart may have been with the major, but she thought her body now belonged to Sher Khan.

Often she had thought of being with him alone, walking down the path which wound its way through the apple and walnut trees to the road head. She imagined sitting with him on the grass beside the stream flowing past her house, listening to his various adventures and tales of far off places. But then, harsh realities would surface, like ugly monsters crushing all her dreams and leaving her heart heavy with despair. He was from a different culture, a different world and most importantly, a different religion. She had often compared the two men in her life, poised on either side of the fence waiting for a chance to kill each other.

The only qualities that the two had in common, were they were both in violent professions, both had a streak of cruelty and in all probability, had the same taste in women. At that, she had smiled to herself.

Perhaps it touched her feminine vanity to see two men 'fight' over her. For she knew that other than the larger issues at stake that brought the two into conflict, she definitely had a hand in adding fuel to the fire of hatred and her female intuition warned her that one of them would definitely not leave the valley alive. With a pang of remorse, she realised that she had more in common with Sher Khan than with Harry.

She had waited for Harry and he hadn't come. Then a few months back, she mustered the courage to go across to meet him. From the villagers she had found out his name and knew that he was stationed in Kuligam in the next valley. So dressed in a black shalwar kameez, with a necklace of old rupee coins which had belonged to her late mother and a few cheap copper rings bought in Kupwara, she had taken the forest short cut which crossed the spur to Moghul Maidan. From there, she had hopped onto the local bus for Kuligam, a mere ten-minute drive.

At the Kuligam post the bus stopped at the barrier and as per the standing instructions of the Army, everybody got down and queued up behind the barrier. A tent fly was pitched next to the sentry post where a drop box had been placed for any local who wanted to pass on information anonymously. Sahira saw Harry sitting on the steps of the verandah deep in conversation with some surrendered militants. She desperately wished he would turn his head and notice her. The queue to the tent got shorter and then she was through and boarding the bus.

Briefly she toyed with the idea of walking up to him. But she realised how fraught with danger the act was, with everybody watching. With a sinking heart, she got into the bus. She could have given him valuable information if only she could meet him. The last she saw of him as the bus moved, was a figure standing on the steps with a radio glued to his ear, looking towards the bus. She raised a tiny hand at the window and waved, but the figure just stood still.

As the days had gone by and Harry hadn't come, she had allowed herself to drift closer to Sher Khan. She knew it was wrong to get involved with a militant, for grief would follow soon. But then Sher Khan was not an easy man to refuse.

Both Harry and Sher Khan were violent, physical men and she wondered why she was drawn to their kind, where grief in the end was clearly written on the wall. She recalled how keen her uncle had been, that she marry his son Taufik, a tailor in the village. She had thrown a huge tantrum at home and had her mother's support. Despite being a girl, she was the only child and quite spoilt. Her poor father had backed off when her mother got personal, citing her own example of marrying the wrong man. She couldn't imagine herself married to the young, spectacled man who made his living stitching people's clothes and barely had the courage to speak to her, when she passed him in the village.

On the other hand, she was drawn to the good-looking Maktub, who was a few years older and looked the kind who would like to protect a woman. Their affair was briefly the talk of the village, before the elders intervened and got them married. They had barely been married a few months when he expressed the desire to fight for jehad and become a mujahid, an idea she rather encouraged and felt proud of.

He had come back a few months later, sunburnt and rugged, brandishing an AK rifle, like a boy with a new toy.

Maktub was dead a few months later, not fighting battles in

the name of Allah, but in an internal skirmish, born of a petty quarrel.

It had been nearly three years since she had thought of a man, and now suddenly, two men had been forced into her life. Why was Allah suddenly playing games with her or was he testing her? Would life have been different if she had married Taufik? Why could the village and the community not produce one soldier like Harry? Perhaps her attraction to such men was the product of having a weak father. All her life she had seen her father bullied, without the moral or physical courage to stand up to anyone. Her poor mother was the real man of the house, and had stood up to society, to protect her. She was the one who had chased away the boys when Sahira was growing up and in her death, had robbed her daughter of a great emotional support.

Maybe she was just looking for someone who could fill her father's shoes and look after her in troubled times.

Harry realised that an ambush could be a delight for a voyeur. He recalled an ambush he had laid a few weeks back, where a woman thinking she was alone on a deserted village path, sat down to pee, not realising that she was barely two metres away from the barrel of the light machine gun. Ten pairs of eyes, with their hearts in their mouths, watched her perform the act, praying that she wouldn't get the urge for something larger and decide to go deeper into the bush.

At about four in the evening Sahira came out carrying some clothes and stood on the verandah. She cast a quick glance at the mountains around and hung a red cloth on the railing of the verandah. Turning suddenly, she walked back, stopped, turned and came back to the other side of the verandah and looked straight towards where the major was hiding a hundred metres uphill, across the stream. She stood still, her gaze fixed for a long time. The major wondered if she had an idea of their presence. He could see the frown on her face, her brow knitted in thought. Then she turned suddenly, as if changing her mind about something she intended to do and disappeared inside.

A little later, the radio crackled to life and Bobby's voice came on the air.

'Two-One, movement eleven o'clock to you, in five one's area, roger that, over.'

'Roger. I see him. Confirmed target,' replied Harry. 'All stations stand by for contact. Five-One, there might be more coming behind him. Your call, take the shot when you are ready.'

Subedar Hari Singh was station Five-One and he was in a bit of a dilemma now. His party had to cover the longest distance, across the stream and then up towards one of the numerous tracks that came down the Khobalmarg top. By the time he arrived at his designated site, it was already getting to be first light. In panic, to salvage the situation, he had tucked his party into the nearest thicket he saw, next to the track. He shouldn't have done so, for the site did not meet even one of the criteria mentioned in the training manuals, essential while selecting an ambush site. He was on a bend and could not cover the area of the track directly above him. His killing area was too close and limited to three metres of the track, running a few metres below and in front. And most importantly, his men had no cover.

He heard the conversation on the radio and was unable to reply for fear of being heard by the mujahid. He couldn't manoeuvre his men to respond to the situation, as the movement of the bushes would be a certain giveaway, inviting fire from the militants, and a burst into the bushes was sure to buy heavy casualties. If the party across did not intervene, he was a dead man. *Subedar* Hari Singh realised two things—the vulnerability of his position and the necessity of divine intervention. His brow wet with cold sweat and his breath frozen on his lips, he did the only thing a man in his position could do. He switched off his radio, motioned to his men to stay still and prayed to Bajrang Bali that the major sahib would understand his predicament.

Harry knew something had gone drastically wrong at Five-One's end. He knew the *subedar* was in danger and in no position to engage the target. In fact, he could guess Hari's location across, and knew the militant would discover them. They were far too close to the track. He took the Drugnov sniper rifle from the soldier next to him and sighted through the high-powered telescope. The man coming down the path was clearly the lead scout, with the main party some distance behind. The mujahid had long hair and a flowing beard, on a face that was cadaverous and acetic. He was a small, thin man and Harry was disappointed that it wasn't Sher Khan walking between the cross of his sights.

The mujahid would take a step, stop, scan the immediate area with the barrel of his weapon always following his gaze. The man was a professional. Harry sighted on the man's head, and then realised that if he missed, he would never be able to forgive himself. But it was more the act of putting a bullet through a face that restrained him. The body seemed a more impersonal target to engage. The muzzle dropped and the sights settled on the middle of the chest. He was aware of five pairs of eyes in the squad watching him. He saw the militant stop short of the bend in the track and go down on the knees to examine something on the ground. He got up and sniffed the air like a gun dog and slowly his weapon came up, swinging menacingly towards the bushes beyond the bend.

Harry knew it was now or never. The militant had either seen the parties' boot marks or had smelt the puri and pickle the men must have eaten for breakfast. Another five steps and he would stumble over Five-One's squad. He told himself to relax, held his breath and squeezed the trigger. The high velocity, seven point six two caliber, steel tipped bullet, travelling at eight hundred metres per second, caught the militant in the centre of the ammunition pouch he was wearing across the chest. The bullet smashed through one of the spare magazines in the pouch and punched a hole below the sternum, exiting from behind his shoulder blade, and leaving a big black gaping hole in its wake.

The impact hurled him back on the track, and he fell as though a mule had kicked him. But he was not dead. Training and survival instincts had taken over in spite of a grievous wound. He immediately rolled over onto his stomach, and through the telescope, Harry saw the eyes alert scan the surroundings in an attempt to identify the direction of fire.

'Take another shot, sahib,' said the man next to Harry.

He fired. Missed and saw dirt kick up five inches to the right of the face. The militant suddenly got up, as if the shot reminded him of his vulnerability and walked three quick steps towards the edge of the track before falling, the body rolling down the steep gradient, to land with a thud on a flat rock, ten metres below. Harry followed the progress of the body in awe. He could not but admire the spirit of the man to live and in that moment of self-preservation, the ability of the mind to select the shortest and the safest route of escape downhill. The macabre dance of death had more to do with years of living dangerously and training, rather than an act of self-preservation, reflected Harry.

The jungle came alive to men, as the ambush was broken. In the village below, people looked up as the first shot reverberated in the valley. Then, like a practiced drill, which comes from having lived in an insurgency environment, the women bundled their kids indoors, those away from their homes sought the shelter of the nearest house and doors and windows were shut. Within minutes, the village wore the look of a deserted town that one sees in western movies, when a gunfight is in the offing.

While Five-One's party dragged the body of the dead militant down to the village, Harry strode purposefully towards Sahira's house, his face a picture of serious reflection, as conflicting emotions ran through his mind. 'Call both of them out', he told one of his men, sitting in front of the house, on a hollowed out trunk used for storing water for the animals. The father walked out, head hanging as if, walking to the gallows and looking more miserable and forlorn than the last time Harry had seen him. He had aged, and guilt was written plainly all over his gaunt face.

Sahira on the other hand, carried herself like a person who was confident in handling the sticky situation, with no trace of the guilt or fear that Harry expected to see on her face. It infuriated Harry even more, to see the woman exuding such confidence after what she had been up to. The least he expected was to see her drop her cocky deportment and look a little worried about her predicament.

For an uncomfortable period, Harry didn't say a word, as both of them stood in front of him, like a couple of naughty kids facing the headmaster. He turned his attention towards the father, completely ignoring Sahira.

'Muhammad Lone, did I not warn you to keep out of this *masla*[2]? Yes or no?' Harry shouted in anger.

The old man nodded with downcast eyes.

'And now you are making money by running your daughter as a whore for the Jehad. Your humble contribution to raise the

[2] An issue

morale of the boys. I am sure,' continued Harry, 'you can offer similar services to the Army. I assure you, we would pay better.'

'*Jenab*,' said Sahira, interjecting.

'Shut up!' Harry shouted her down. 'You have forfeited the right to be treated with respect as a woman, you whore of Lolab. And because I can't make you pay for what you are up to, we will straighten your old man out, for producing a loose bitch like you. Come on old man,' he indicated, with a nod of his head. 'Let's give you some army hospitality long overdue.'

The old man mumbled something about not knowing what his daughter was up to, and realising that no one was even listening to him and that any further excuses would be futile, he followed the column of men trudging down the track towards the vehicle pick-up point. Harry looked at the dead militant whose body had been dragged down, and was now strapped to a charpoy. He examined the body to see where he had collected the bullet. It surprised him how such a thin man could have moved with such a fatal shot. The bullet had punched through the ammunition pouch across his chest as he had seen through the telescope and torn a hole the size of a fist in the back on its exit. He winched thinking how it would feel to get shot. Just looking at the dead man gave him a tremendous high—his adrenaline was still running.

This definitely went right up in the list of the most satisfying achievements one could have, he thought. From a six, sailing over the bowlers head in cricket to a right and left shot in a partridge shoot, or a punch to the jaw of your opponent in boxing to see him pole axed straight to the canvas, or for that matter, scaling a summit. But this was way beyond any experience. The blood lust disturbed him a trifle and he wondered if this was the kind of addiction which drove thugs to kill in the name of Kali. He recalled reading about a chap called Ameer Ali, who with a favourite thug weapon, the *rumal*[3], strangulated nearly seven hundred and nineteen people in the eighteenth century. And as he confessed in captivity to his jailors, if he hadn't been in jail for twelve years, his tally would have crossed a thousand.

There was a short story he had read once, about a well-known, English big-game hunter in the early nineteenth century, who fell off a ship one night and swam ashore to a small, thickly forested island. There was a single dim light in the distance and he followed it to arrive at a huge mansion. He was taken in by the servant and entertained very warmly by the owner, a very aristocratic, middle-aged Russian. Apparently, there were only the two of them in the house, or for that matter on the island, which happened to be owned by the Russian and attended to by his dumb and deaf servant. There were animal trophies of all kinds displayed in the house; on the walls, the shelves everywhere. Over drinks the host talked about his experience of big-game hunting across the world and was eager for his guest's view, aware of his guest's reputation as one of the best big-game hunters in the world.

'Well, allow me to disagree', said the Russian, when told by his guest that in his opinion the most dangerous game was an angry African bison. 'As you can see, I have hunted almost every kind of animal there is to hunt and have come to the conclusion, that the most dangerous and exciting game to hunt is—man.' The guest is thereafter, let loose on the island while the Russian and his servant track their quarry. The story ends with the Englishman finally turning the tables and killing the Russian and his servant.

Harry could completely relate to the Russian in the story. He had once tracked a wounded militant and it was one of the most

[3] Handkerchief

nerve-racking and exciting experiences of his life. Of course, Harry was fortunate that the man had covered half a kilometre and then probably out of exhaustion from blood loss, had decided to make a last stand. He died before he could inflict any damage and was found with his head resting on his rifle, in the lee of a huge deodar tree, covering the path that his pursuers were following. Harry, being in the lead, was definitely a dead man if the militant had just stayed alive a few more minutes. He was drenched in sweat by the time he finished and was certain he had lost a couple of pounds. Once the act of killing is justified and your conscious is clean, realised Harry, there is a distinct flavour to the experience, which over time can become addictive.

'Who is this man?' asked Harry, turning to Sahira. 'Another one of your lovers?'

'He is no lover of mine,' she replied, with a touch of anger in her voice. 'They called him Rashid and that's all I know.'

Harry pulled out a blood-soiled letter from the dead man's pocket. It was in Urdu and written by Rashid to his mother and carried a Karachi address. He asked Sahira to read it. The letter generally talked about how well he was and what a fine job he was doing in the name of Allah. It ended on a pompous note of how his name was feared amongst the Security Forces and the high esteem he was held in, amongst his mujahidin brothers.

Harry pondered for some time and then asked Sahira to write the following at the end of the page in Urdu.

'Your son Rashid was shot dead on the 23 November in a place called the Lolab Valley, (Gagal village) Kashmir India. He died fighting like a true mujahid. The letter was found in his pocket and I am posting it on his behalf. *Khuda hafiz*. Signed, An Indian Army Officer.'

'Now,' he said turning back to Sahira, 'what should we do with you, my pretty slut?'

It was taking a lot of effort on Harry's part to control the urge to inflict pain. He knew he was using harsh language, but he felt betrayed and cheated. It was a typical male ego thing over a female and his ego was hurt. Sher Khan had got the fair girl. He could see Sahira wanted to say something but was holding herself back. She didn't know him well enough to open up, or perhaps it was because there were so many soldiers around. It never struck him that Sahira had known of the presence of soldiers in the undergrowth across the house all along. She had come back from meeting Sher Khan and found the cattle to be uneasy, the conspicuous silence of bird chatter and the faint glint of sunlight reflecting off glass or metal in the bushes. She knew immediately it was the army and a strange intuition told her it was Harry and his men.

Harry saw tears well up in her eyes and he immediately felt sorry. It struck him that if he wanted to win her he should have been bolder. He had a strong urge to take her in his arms and comfort her, but knew he could never do so in front of the men he commanded. God, he thought. I am definitely falling in love with this girl. He shouted for the *subedar* to release Sahira's father and told the men to march back to the vehicles. He was the last to leave and under the big walnut tree that lead to the entrance of her house, he turned and looked at Sahira.

It was a look between a man and a woman where words are not necessary. They looked into each other and discovered feelings that had remained unexpressed. For some strange reason, Harry knew that it was probably going to be a long time before he would set eyes on her again, and he felt certain that the circumstances would change. In spite of poverty, she managed to be well dressed and kept her surroundings clean. She could read and write which was rare for a Gujjar woman and had shown keen interest in most of the subjects that he often talked about. She was undoubtedly a good woman. There was something eternally sad, appealing and beautiful about the woman, with her haunting dark eyes, moist with tears and pouting red lips quivering with emotion, a red scarf covering her long, thick hair. The picture of her like this would remain with him forever.

He felt a pang of jealousy and regret that he would never be able to make love to her, while another man—a bloody militant!—had had that opportunity. He wondered why he was drawn emotionally to her in spite of huge differences. Maybe his last experience with a woman had left a bad taste in the mouth. He recalled Tina, a tall, beautiful girl many years younger than him. They had briefly dated and felt sufficiently in love to tie the knot. She had called off the engagement barely four months later, while he was away climbing. Harry had received the 'Dear John' letter at the Nanda Devi base camp.

Tina had been a highly ambitious woman, glamour struck and hungry for recognition. Harry, as a soldier, was like the proverbial square peg in a round hole for her and the relationship was doomed even before it had begun. She had walked out on him for a model; after all, they made a nice picture for some of the Page 3 parties in town. It had left Harry a little unsure and bitter against big city girls, and he could completely relate to Sahira's simplicity and admire her strength and struggle in life.

Harry took a couple of hundred rupee notes out of his pocket and placed it on a rock under the tree and then, as an afterthought, he took off his lucky Ganesha gold chain from around his neck—a gift from his mother—and placed it over the notes.

'May it bring you good fortune, Sahira,' he said, and giving her one last look, he turned and went down the path, after his retreating men.

Shumrial Village

A Few Months later | (1700 hrs)

Lu Sangu Lava Lu Sangu.
'Blood washes Blood.'

—Sicilian Proverb

Javed Jabbar, the psycho ex-barber turned battalion commander, paced up and down in front of the two villagers who had been quarrelling over a land issue. They now stood silently as Javed gave them his unwanted advice. They had been arguing, when suddenly Javed had imposed himself as a self-appointed arbitrator and they were only too aware of his unpredictable reputation, to tell him to mind his own business. They were saved when the proceedings were interrupted by a foreign militant.

'Javed bhai,' he said, 'Sher Khan has asked for a bag of flour, and some eggs and chicken to be sent up to the hideout.'

Javed didn't like being interrupted, especially when he was dealing with people. He hoped one day, when all this militancy was over, to stand for elections. It wasn't a far-fetched dream. Enough criminals and dacoits were getting tickets from established parties, so why not him? In fact, there was already a well-known ex-militant who was now a local politician from the Bandipore constituency and he was lending all his support to the army against militancy. His boys now carried out road-opening duties for the army convoys. He had never believed in any sort of freedom for Kashmir. Militancy was an opportunity, a God-sent chance to make money and indulge in crime which came easily to him, and he had grabbed it.

Just a few years back, Javed was shaving beards and cutting hair in a shop in Kupwara—a nobody who was in love with a pretty Kashmiri girl. But both father and girl were dead against him. They thought he was too low down in the social ladder other than his reputation for criminal activity. He was known to have a police record for various crimes, including an attempted murder with a cut-throat razor. The Jehad had changed the equation completely. Once back from Pakistan with a weapon, the first thing he did was to eliminate both the girl he loved and her father. Their bodies were found floating in the Lolab River with their throats slit. No evidence was ever found, but everybody in the village knew who had done it. Javed's reputation as a cold killer was established.

He was polite to the foreign militants to the extent that he realised his salary, ammunition, weapons, etc. depended on them. However today, he lost it. Especially after the way Sher Khan had conducted himself during the killing of Alia Chopan. There was mutual dislike between them. There was so much arrogance in him, thought Javed, as though he and his guest mujahidin were Allah's own gift to jehad and a local militant could not be trusted to fight! Absolutely insulting and on top of it, they were philandering around with the women! If Sher Khan as the leader could get himself a mistress, what about his other hired henchmen and their behaviour with the local women? They were here to fight a jehad, not to party and womanise.

'Sure,' he snapped irritated, 'I hope you are carrying money. Pay and by all means eat whatever you want to. But if you don't intend to pay, then I suggest you tell Sheru bhai to make do with the usual dal-roti.'

The man was taken aback and more surprised than hurt. He couldn't understand what had come over Javed to be so insulting. No Kashmiri mujahid would dare speak like this to a foreign fighter. Everybody knew the power to hold the Jehad together was in their hands. They controlled the purse strings and the local mujahid was supposed to dance to their tune.

'Fine, *jenab*' he said 'I will convey your sentiments to Sheru bhai. However, as someone who has been your brother in arms, I would advise discretion in your speech with Sher Khan.' And with that he turned and walked back up.

Quick to anger, Javed also cooled down pretty fast and now, with his anger gone, he knew he had pushed his luck too far this time. He immediately started shouting at the some of the locals standing around to organise the foodstuff. Javed had barely managed to get everything together when he heard footsteps coming down the path and sure enough, Sher Khan, his eyes blazing, strode up to him with his two Paki pals, Gul and Malik, following behind. Javed's first reaction was that Sher Khan would lash out with his hands and foot and so he turned a little to the side to present a smaller target. But Sher Khan had other ways of sorting out insubordination.

Sher Khan stood looking down into Javed's eyes for some time, as though wondering what punishment should merit the insult, while the latter stood rooted to the spot knowing that he was as close to death as he could be. Sher Khan would often say a man's life was cheaper than the price of a chicken in this country and these were people and places that went beyond the laws of the land. Javed braced himself for the punch or the bullet, but neither came. Instead, in a very gentle voice, Sher Khan instructed him to take his clothes and shoes off.

'No...no, *jenab*,' pleaded Javed, knowing that humiliation was what Sher Khan had in mind. 'Shoot me instead.'

'Did you give me a choice when you insulted me, Javed? We haven't come all this way and taken huge risks to be insulted by you people,' replied Sher Khan. 'Now pick up all the stuff on your head and walk up to the hideout in your underwear. You are lucky there is no donkey handy or I would have shown you how we treat people like you back home in my village. Let the locals also see what a great mujahid you are.'

Javed was seething with anger and humiliation as he carried the sack of flour on his back, while Sher Khan and his cronies walked behind, cracking jokes and laughing at his expense.

'How much do you want us to pay you for donkey services?' asked one of them, laughing. 'Next time you will probably ask for rent for staying in a jungle hideout too! Amazing!' he continued, shaking his head in disbelief. 'Imagine asking us to pay for fighting your war. We, who are your guests. What is this—a jehad or a bloody business opportunity for making money? We are mujahidin, brother, and your guests, not tourists.'

With grim satisfaction, Sher Khan looked at the thin, naked figure struggling along, bent under the weight of the sack. The lesson was plain enough, he thought, and the message clear. No messing with the foreign mujahidin. But little did he know that in the sly-looking Javed, he had made a bitter foe.

After forty minutes of climbing and just a hundred metres short of the ridgeline, they arrived at a small gully. A thin trickle of water, from the accumulated snow further up the mountain dropped hesitatingly in a mini waterfall, to make a small pool next to a circle of boulders. A three by three metre hole dug between the boulders, covered with a tin roof and camouflaged with dirt and shrubs, served as a hideout. A small hole next to the rocks, with a few steps, led into the damp interior. A dull wicker lamp placed in a niche, cast grotesque shadows around a room high enough for a midget. A normal man had to practically bend his back to move around.

The floor was covered with dry grass; the mattresses and quilts had been rolled and neatly tucked in one corner, while rations in tins and other assortment of utensils, occupied the opposite corner. The floor was wet in places where water had been dripping from the roof and the place smelt of unwashed clothes, sweat and damp earth. It was a hard place to live and had to be, for it was designed for hard, desperate men, and served as a winter hideout.

Javed, with an aching back, heaved a sigh of relief as he threw the sack off and dragged it into the hideout.

'My clothes, *jenab*,' he asked Sher Khan, looking miserable and shivering in the evening cold.

Sher Khan looked at one of the foreign fighters, who tossed the clothes at Javed along with his rifle. Leaving a man outside as a sentry, the rest of the group went down into the hideout. Javed, still seething with anger, found himself a corner and sat sulking quietly through the proceedings. Sher Khan talked about the new set of orders he had received from his handlers in Pakistan once the snow melted. The fight now had to be taken to the kafirs, and their posts, their convoys and their patrols had to be attacked. Escalate the conflict and let the Indians commit more troops and resources. Bleed them militarily and financially.

He saw Javed sitting quietly in a dark corner. In the faded half light Sher Khan could not see the expression of sheer hatred and anger on Javed's face as he sat working himself up for retaliation. Something had to be done or else he would never be able to face the villagers. His reputation was at stake.

'Come on brother,' said Sher Khan addressing Javed, realising he had been a bit too harsh and the act may have offended other local fighters too. 'No hard feelings among the mujahidin,' he continued, 'I have already forgotten the transgression, so let's go out and offer namaz.'

With that Sher Khan got up and walked out, followed by the others. Javed was the last to leave. He lingered just a little longer to allow the rest of them to get out and then very quietly, cocked his weapon, switching the lever to automatic fire. When he emerged outside the sun was going down the Gagal ridgeline and the various nooks and corners of the jungle were already in shadows. In a few minutes, darkness would descend. He saw the mujahidin facing west, their backs towards him. Sher Khan was the last in line.

Javed Jabbar had a fleeting moment of panic at what he was about to do and then his pent up rage took possession of him. He saw the tall figure of Sher Khan with his hands cupped behind his ears and without taking proper aim, he squeezed the trigger. But Sher Khan's time had not come yet, and by sheer coincidence he had bowed in prayer to his maker as the bullets missed his head. In his fear and excitement, with shaking hands, Javed had fired too high and the automatic mode kicked the weapon further away from Sher Khan. The bullets hit the rock in front and ricocheted, with one of them finding its target, ripping through Sher Khan's left arm and severing an artery.

Javed only had a glimpse of Sher Khan clutching his arm and rolling over as he turned and disappeared downhill at a run. Within seconds, he was swallowed by the gathering darkness.

He had grown up in these mountains and knew Sher Khan and his foreign cronies could spend the rest of their lives looking for him, without ever finding him. The local fighters would definitely not give away one of their Kashmiri brethren and all he had to do was get away to another area. He crossed the Kupwara-Lolab road and started his climb towards Kalaruch.

With danger far behind, Javed Jabbar smiled in the darkness. He berated himself for not aiming properly and knew that he had positively hit Sher Khan. He pleaded to Allah to make the wound a fatal one. Either way, he knew the whole bunch of them would be fuming. It was probably the first time a local mujahid had fired upon a guest fighter, and that too, a senior commander!

Back at the hideout after the initial shock, things were coming under control. Sher Khan had been pulled inside and someone was trying to stop the incessant, heavy bleeding with some dirty cloth torn from one of the militant's shirt. Sher Khan sat stoically, his gaze fixed at the dim flickering lamp light. Gul could be heard outside, cursing and abusing the Kashmiri militants in Punjabi. A local fighter was dispatched immediately to go down to the village and fetch a *hakim*. The flow of blood had to be stopped, or Sher Khan might die by morning.

Sher Khan found it difficult to keep his eyes open and had a strong desire to sleep. He was finding it difficult to focus on the flickering lamp, which seemed to dance and multiply. He had seen enough gunshot wounds to know from experience that the extensive loss of blood was making him slowly lose consciousness. In the absence of medical treatment, if he closed his eyes, he would probably never open them again.

The pain came in waves. Beginning somewhere in and around the wound like an innocent irritation, it would gather momentum and size and consume his whole body, till nothing else existed. And just as suddenly and intensely as it had grown, it would release its grip, leaving the body to recoup and prepare itself for the next assault. Sher Khan knew he had to fight this pain and keep awake and alert. He pulled his radio set out and called for all stations in the Lolab Valley.

Company Post–Kuligam Village
(1900 HRS)

Every man dies, but not every man truly lives.
—Pakistani Proverb

HARRY AND BOBBY were briefing the company cook on how to prepare a duck that had been presented by a villager. Operations had slowed down with the onset of winter and one had more time to spend at the post. Other than women, food occupied a large part of a soldier's imagination. The *bukhari* was glowing and the room was nice and warm. They sat, watching a Madhuri Dixit movie on TV, when suddenly instead of Madhuri dancing to the tune of *Ek-do-teen*[1], they heard the heavy familiar voice of Sher Khan.

'Shit!' exclaimed Harry. 'I can't even watch a movie in peace. Bloody TV is also catching radio transmissions. Switch it off Bobby and turn on the radio set. Sher Khan at this late hour could mean that something is brewing.'

The radio on intercept mode automatically locked on to the most powerful frequency and the voice became clearer and louder.

[1] Literal meaning, one, two, three; a popular Bollywood song of the late 1980s.

'Hey, there is something wrong sir,' said Bobby. 'He is sounding tired and there is a bit of wheezing. Can you hear the long pauses between sentences, as if it is a strain to talk? And no other station seems to be engaging him, it is all one sided, more like a soliloquy…' Both officers pulled their chairs closer to the radio and waited.

'We came here to fight,' continued Sher Khan, 'against a kafir nation which has been subjugating the Kashmiris for so long and what do we get in return but a thankless bunch of people. What the barber did today and I won't repeat it, for I am aware the army dogs are also listening, is something which is going to cost some people very dearly.'

There was a long pause and Bobby took the opportunity to throw some wood into the *bukhari* while Harry quickly refilled his drink.

'Something's up,' said Bobby. 'The guy sounds tired and emotional. They generally go off the air by this time and the fact that he is on the radio now and not really speaking to anyone in particular, my guess, boss, is that most of the stations in the Lolab are tuned in. The guy is pissed off big time about something.'

'To those who think I will lose my grip,' continued Sher Khan, 'because of this incident, are in for a disappointment. What is meant to flow is flowing and the guns which were meant for the kafirs, can in no time be turned. You are either with us or against us and if the latter—then we will paint the valley red.'

'Wow!' said Harry beaming. 'I think they are fighting amongst themselves. He is clearly threatening the local militant cadres with dire consequences. I wonder why? You heard what he said about "what is meant to flow is flowing". I bet he is wounded and bleeding!'

'What fun!' said Bobby, getting up and pouring himself a drink. 'We just need to monitor the situation and see the opportunity to insert ourselves somewhere.'

'You are celebrating too soon,' replied Harry. 'Sher Khan carries the purse and the local militants have no choice but to dance to his tune. This will all settle down in a few days. The good news is that it gives us some respite. They won't be up to any mischief for some time now.'

'I said it before and will say it again,' the voice sounded dull and extremely tired. 'Hand over the man responsible for this incident and we will forget and move on. You have five days to get your hands on him, or else I will issue fresh instructions to the guest mujahidin.'

'*Mohataram*,' piped up a scared, hesitant voice. The accent was Kashmiri and the voice sounded far away. 'Don't judge us all by one man's action. While we will make our best efforts, how can we find him in five days, *jenab*? He could be anywhere from here to Muzaffrabad!'

There was a long pause. The radio silence was finally broken by Malik.

'We don't care, brother,' he said, the anger in his voice quite noticeable. 'If anything happens to Sheru bhai, we will forget what we are here for and there will be hell to pay. So while you find the traitor, make sure you find a good doctor as well before that. *Khuda hafiz*.'

Both officers waited for some time and realised that the curtain was finally down on the evening's entertainment.

'Keep your eyes and ears open and spread the word about any doctors being moved around. Let's also try and piece the story together. Find out who shot Sher Khan and maybe we have an important ally in this fight,' said Harry.

Shumrial Village
(A MONTH LATER) | (0930 HRS)

Time is like a sword. If you do not cut it, it will cut you.
—Arabic Proverb

AN UN-METALLED ROAD running north east from the frontier town of Kupwara enters the Lolab Valley. Two kilometres from the town, the road passes the *Pir Baba*'s *ziarat*[1], adorned with numerous green banners presented as offering by the various army units which served in the area. On the left, the ridgeline climbs up supporting on its lower shoulder, the village of Khanakund before rising to a great height, beyond which lies the village of Kalaruch. On either side of the road, lie the twin villages of Khumrial and Shumrial.

While the former is densely packed along the road, the latter village is across the Lolab River, tucked in the folds of thickly wooded mountains. In army parlance, Shumrial was a 'black' village, as the locals in a majority were pro-militancy. As it saddled the narrowest point at the *Pir Baba*'s *ziarat*, where the mountains where barely three hundred metres apart, the village was strategic

[1] Islamic shrine

to facilitate north-south militant movement. The river in front and the surrounding mountains gave it natural protection from any military operation. From the *ziarat*, the valley opened out to encompass the entire stretch of land called the south Lolab Basin.

Sher Khan looked out of the window at the thick snowflakes floating earthwards and reflexively pulled himself closer to the log fire in the hearth. He wrapped the blanket tighter, wincing in pain in the attempt. After the shootout, he had immediately been carried to the village of Shumrial where a local doctor had crudely stitched up his wound. He had remained comatose for three days and was even now, finding it difficult to walk on his own steam. Sahira had been around to nurse him and one of the foreign militants was always in the house as a bodyguard. The incident had changed Sher Khan, for he now seemed to have lost all faith in the Kashmiris. A certain arrogant rudeness was noticeable in the way he addressed the locals and the brunt of his insults was directed at none other than Sahira.

The disdain which he had always felt for the locals now emerged and he made no attempt at hiding his feelings. A local militant came to report to him, and he snapped irritably, 'Go ask the army or Javed, that hero of yours who is still absconding. If you guys were serious, you would have produced Javed by now. None of you are interested in *aazadi*. We are wasting our time here.'

Sahira, who had nursed him all along, expected some gratitude instead of the constant barbs he threw at her. She represented the race and thereby all that Sher Khan abhorred about the Kashmiris and his spite came out on her. He was an outdoor man and his confinement, injury and the damp, cold weather only added to his frustration. Since his injury, the momentum once again seemed to have gone out and all militant activity had come to a standstill.

Sher Khan was coming under pressure from his handlers across the border to revive and up the ante. 'Keep the kettle boiling,' he was constantly reminded, 'but don't let the water spill over.'

Sher Khan fixed the date and called for a meeting of all senior militant cadres in the Lolab Valley.

Army Post–Kuligam Village
(0700 HRS)

A desk is a dangerous place from which to view the world.
—John le Carré

HARRY WAS LYING in his sleeping bag, mustering courage to get out, for the cold was bone-numbing. He looked at the *bukhari* expectantly, imagining its warmth when lit. His underwear and socks were spread on the wooden chair and instinctively he pulled them into the sleeping bag to warm before slipping them on. A cold draught from the window hit his face and managed to slip into his sleeping bag before he could zip it. He shivered and looked out. Most of the window panes were broken or cracked and an attempt to cover the open ones with newspaper had failed, as some had now come off and were fluttering in the breeze. There was a full-fledged blizzard blowing outside. Some bloody paradise, thought Harry.

There was a knock and the intelligence havildar entered and saluted. He handed Harry a slip of paper.

'This was in the information drop box, sahib,' he said. 'Probably, someone who came by in the half-empty morning bus. There has been no other movement in this weather.'

Harry handed it back to the havildar and asked him to read it, for the letter was written in Urdu. It was addressed to the Company Commander-Kuligam Post.

Mohataram asalaam-walekum.

I hope by Allah's grace you are in good health. You and I have one common objective and that is to see Sher Khan dead.

'Stop,' Harry said, 'just go across and call Bobby sahib to join me here and tell Balwant to fire up the *bukhari*. Nobody is going out anywhere in this weather.'

'Continue,' he told the havildar, once Bobby had made himself comfortable in one of the chairs. 'I think we are on to something important here,' he said turning to him. The havildar continued.

As you read this letter, Sher Khan is sitting in the village of Shumrial, recuperating from a wound. A wound to say the least, this writer has a hand in. He has called for a salah mashwara[1] *ten days from now. If* jenab *can hit the village before azan,* Insha' Allah, *Sher Khan might find himself a permanent resting place six feet under.* Khuda Hafiz.

'Now what do you make of it?' asked Harry. 'I think it's the barber waiting for a chance to strike back.'

'I agree, boss,' replied Bobby. 'The mention of the writer having a hand in wounding Sher Khan, indicates our psycho friend. And he has been missing from the area for a long time after the shootout. Let's hope the weather clears—I don't fancy going into action in this kind of poor visibility. The choppers can't land in case of a casualty. And incidentally, why don't you keep your room a little cozier sir? I just can't understand this self-

[1] Discussion

inflicted punishment. I mean you are not on Nanda Devi, for God's sake!'

'Well to be honest,' replied Harry, 'with all the high altitude climbing, one would think I probably enjoy an outing in this weather. But given a chance I would love to spend my time in front of a fire reading a book. But then, as they say in our trade… The desk is a dangerous place to view the world from.'

Ill Met In Shumrial
(0200 HRS)

My centre is giving way, my right is retreating,
situation excellent, I am attacking.

—Ferdinand Foch

IN THE WEAK moonlight, the landscape looked like a child's black and white drawing with a road, trees, snow, and the dark silhouette of the mountains on either side. The convoy with its headlights off, roared past the village of Khumrial on their way to Kupwara. At the *ziarat,* a few vehicles stopped briefly and about twenty men and both the officers got off. The plan was to drive the game, if the information was correct, to the guns. While multiple ambushes were to be thrown around the village of Shumrial, the remaining troops would return in the morning and advance openly towards the village for a search and destroy mission. Or, it was hoped, drive the militants in the village to seek the sanctuary of the jungles around and into the waiting ambush parties.

Bobby stamped his feet and pulled on his gloves. He saw the men huddled at the side of the road in the shadows. The slush on the road was worse than the snow and two pairs of Siachen socks and the standard Indian army rubber snow boots weren't good enough to keep toes warm. The temperature must have been minus ten and the silent houses in the darkness looked inviting. Bobby walked up to Harry who was in conversation with the men.

'You command the party on the east of the village and I will make a full circuit and be just opposite you on the other side of the village,' said Harry. 'The main nala needs a few people but I guess we have no more troops.'

They went down to the Lolab River avoiding the houses. The bridge looked tempting but Harry knew they would leave footprints in the snow. The game would be up even before it had started. He stood looking at the shallow river mustering his courage to wade in. Getting your socks wet and then lasting it out in an ambush in snow, was going to be a miserable experience. He had lost toes on the Nanda Devi climb, and worried about exposing the remaining to another ordeal. Bobby walked up to him from behind.

'Sir, not a good idea,' he whispered. 'Bad start with wet feet, the boys will not be able to sit tight if the cold gets to them and that'll be the end of your surprise.'

'Heard, considered and overruled,' said Harry. 'Now Bobby, get on with the job.'

Having crossed the river, the party skirted the village, keeping to the high up parts of the jungle. The cross-country movement in the thick snow was a nightmare, but the exercise kept the body warm and took the mind off cold feet. At five in the morning, Harry confirmed to Bobby that he was in position. Four ambush parties were covering the most probable routes along some of the smaller gullies and spurs coming down into the village that the militants might take as they ran out. The village below looked peaceful and quiet. A narrow nala which saw a healthy stream in the summertime, ran through the middle of the village to join the main river below. Any onlooker gazing at the serene setting below would have found it difficult to imagine the violence that was brewing.

At six in the morning most of the village was still asleep. A rooster crowed somewhere and the first of the chimneys came alive. White smoke spiralled upwards lazily, disappearing into a thin mist which still hung low over the village. Someone coughed, gargled and cleared his throat in the distance and then set about chopping wood. In another hour, the sun would break through the morning mist to provide much needed warmth and life would resume its hustle and bustle for the day. For the waiting men in the bushes, it had been a hard night and the faint rumble of vehicles in the distance meant the beginning, of the end of a nasty operation. Harry exchanged a look with his signal operator who went on the net, had a brief chat and nodded to him.

'The party under Prakash sahib has arrived,' he said. 'They are splitting into two columns and will advance up the village on either side of the nala in front.'

'Right. Inform all stations the search has started and to be alert. Good hunting.'

Sher Khan was fast asleep when his radio came alive and simultaneously his bodyguard rushed into the room in panic.

'Sheru bhai, it's a crack down! The army is coming in for a search!'

Sher Khan moved with an alacrity which came from having spent years in such environments. He wore his ammunition pouch, picked up his weapon and was ready for departure before Sahira could even realise that he was not in bed.

'You stay here,' he looked at her, 'and when all this is over I will send for you.' In the half light, Sher Khan was suddenly and strangely struck by her beauty. She looked tired and concerned.

What a day for Allah to desert us, he thought. Most of the top commanders in the Lolab were in the village. To fight would be foolhardy. Losing all the commanders would be a huge setback. He went on the radio and spoke to Malik.

'You know the drill. Tell Gul and Badshah to engage from either sides of the village. That should put a stop to their advance. Inform all other brothers to make their way out. Once we have height, we will give covering fire for the two of them to escape.'

While Gul and Badshah were making their way to the end of the village, the other militants who had split up and spent the night in various houses spread across the periphery of the village, selected the dips and folds of the ground to gain the safe sanctuary of the bordering jungle. The first lot ran into Bobby's party. Suddenly the early morning calm was shattered by loud gunfire. The sound sent a shiver of excitement up Harry's spine and his adrenaline went on overdrive. All his senses were suddenly honed, the night's fatigue gone, and the discomfort to toes forgotten. He was not living anymore, he was alive. Harry looked across the village and guessed it was Bobby engaging. Through the field glass he saw a brown ragged figure in *phiran* hugging the ground and trying to crawl into a nala.

'Bobby, if you can hear me,' Harry went on the net, 'one of the buggers is in the nala below you and trying to get back into the village. Toss a few grenades.'

Then, the jungle to the right of Bobby erupted in gunfire and simultaneously, the party to Harry's left, joined the chorus. There was pandemonium in the village below. The path running in the middle, along the now frozen stream, was full of panic-stricken men and women seeking the shelter of their houses. God, thought Harry. Three out of four ambushes had struck gold. What a day. He looked at his four men and told them to be sharp. He knew the militants were trying to break the cordon to escape and that it was just a matter of time before they would select the only route which seemed to have been quiet so far. He looked at the dwindling stream of people below and wondered how many were innocent villagers and how many were militants. The advantage was always with the militants, for the rules of engagement were very clear from the army's side—either you see the weapon on the person or you are fired upon and till then, you control your trigger finger. Following the orders had cost the army some good men over the years.

The mayhem below must have gone on for barely five minutes when at the entrance to the village, a fierce gun battle irrupted. A panic-stricken Prakash sahib was panting and shouting in the radio, asking for reinforcements.

'I am pinned down, Two-One!' he screamed calling Harry. 'Fire from all sides and I am finding it difficult to advance.'

'Prakash sahib,' Harry's calm voice came across loud and clear. 'Stop screaming! What reinforcements? You are the reinforcement. I can tell you from this distance that there are only two rifles and they are moving around to confuse you. Standard practice in built up area, sahib. So get your act together and start manoeuvring or you will be sitting on your arse the whole day.'

Sher Khan and his bodyguard had decided to follow the group who were climbing the spur, very close to the house where they had spent the night. They had barely gone a hundred yards, when the mountainside in front came alive to the hollow bark of AK rifle fire, and he saw the mujahids scatter. He was experienced enough to know immediately that the village was surrounded and that the clever thing to do was to wait and watch, instead of seeking the safety of the jungle in a panic. Sure enough, his patience paid off as the firing disclosed the position of the various parties.

He joined a stream of panic-stricken locals and ran uphill towards the opposite end of the village. At the edge of the main nala coming down from the heights, he dashed into the last house to plan his next move. From the window on the first floor he surveyed the scene. Sporadic gunfire was still heard from the surrounding jungle, but it was the ferocious battle raging at the entrance to the village, that drew his attention. He knew Gul and Badshah were making their presence felt.

He called Gul on the radio and asked him to pull out.

'Sheru bhai, I am wounded,' came the terse strained reply. 'My time has come, do remember me in your blessings,' and then Sher Khan heard the mutterings of a *kalma*, '....Bismallah-a-ra...' The sound became a garbled whisper and finally drowned in a fresh burst of loud gunfire.

'Gul, Gul, do you hear me?' Sher Khan was practically pleading. 'I am coming down, you need to get out...And where is Badshah? Ask him to give you covering fire!' There was silence for some time and then the faint voice of Gul came on the line again.

'Badshah is *shaheed*, *Khuda hafiz*.' And the radio went dead.

In the village below, Harry had joined Prakash sahib, and was directing the villagers out of the fire zone in one of the side lanes. There were old men and women in burkha, with frightened children clutching their robes, trying to vacate the houses and get out of harm's way. Sahira had also joined the procession and was heading out with the throng when she saw Harry standing in the corner. His beard was trimmed and he looked leaner and handsomer than she last remembered him. She had a strong urge to throw off her veil and walk up to him, but knew it was fraught with danger. She was a mujahid's mistress now and a source of information to the army. Even if Harry didn't want to, he would be forced to send her to the joint interrogation cell or some other such place that she had heard such horrid tales about. Everybody was aware that she had eloped with Sher Khan and was a wanted person.

She found it difficult to move from the spot, until she noticed Harry waving at her to move on. With a heavy heart, she turned the corner on her way across the river. She crossed the bridge and briefly stood looking back, with a prayer on her lips for Harry's safety. It struck her as strange that not once had she thought about Sher Khan's survival. Maybe he came across as the kind who could look after himself in rough places and Harry with his sad eyes aroused maternal feelings. In a few minutes, she was on the road and the sound of gunfire and the madness of the moment were fading behind her.

Meanwhile Badshah was surrounded in a house and Harry had managed to talk him into allowing the residents to vacate, before bringing heavy fire on the house. He had stood in the corner urging all the women and kids to clear the area, when he noticed the woman in the light blue burkha. Something about her seemed familiar, or was he imagining things? All women in burkha looked the same. He waved for her to move, saw the hesitation and the thought struck him that maybe she wanted to share some information. There was a burst of gunfire and the next instant when he turned, she was gone. Bobby walked up and saw Harry smiling.

'Well, what's up sir?' he asked, ducking his head as a bullet whined overhead. 'You seem to be amused about something in this tamasha.'

'Oh, just a stupid joke I remembered, seeing all these women running around like headless chicken,' he answered, leaning against the wall. 'Might as well share it with you. Under the circumstances, who knows, I might never get the chance.'

'In a war, the enemy soldier captures three women. I want revenge, he screams, so I am going to screw the three of you. "No, no!" pleads one of the young women. "Have us but please spare the old woman." "Shut up," snaps the old woman, "—war is war."

'You and your intellectual jokes, sir,' answered Bobby. 'Right, can I give you the low down on the action? I think the party is coming to an end. There is intermittent firing from the house and in all probability, it's the same guy engaging us from different positions. Suggest firing a rocket into the house. The longer this firing continues, the greater are the chances of someone collecting lead—law of averages.'

'Law of averages or law of a firefight,' replied Harry. Suddenly the firing picked up again and from a different quarter. Someone came on the set calling for Harry. 'Sanjay is hit, Sanjay is hit!,' the voice kept repeating. Harry and Bobby exchanged a look and ran towards the sound of firing.

'Hope it's not Sanju Baba from seven platoon,' exclaimed Harry. 'He is too young to die. This must be the other bugger, but I thought we had neutralized him.'

'You know what the crafty bastard did?' answered Bobby, panting. 'He went quiet and while the other guy engaged us, he slipped out and got into another house. The usual game of mutual fire support and extraction.'

'And I won't be surprised,' replied Harry, 'if the bunch that got away opens up on us from the heights.'

It was young Sanju all right, but it was a relief to see him walking on his own feet. His jaw was crudely bandaged and he seemed to be more in shock than pain. The latter would of course, follow later. The bullet meant for his heart, had grazed the top edge of his bulletproof vest, been reflected and viciously smashed his jaw in the bargain. Harry saw a few of his men were pinned down in a shallow ditch and the only cover available was a thin wooden palisade running around the house, that was not good enough to stop the bullets Gul was raining on them.

The first round from the eighty-four millimetre Karl Gustav went through the wooden house to explode harmlessly across the mountain. The next was a beauty and blew Gul to his maker in a state that even his mother wouldn't have been able to recognise. The first floor collapsed and Gul's burnt and shattered body was flung out. His legs were stuck under the debris and the other half of the body with its charred face, hung out. Someone fired a few shots into him out of rage, and then stopped, realising the futility of wasted ammunition. He was as dead as a door nail. Harry patted the young gunner for a good shot.

'Hope the bastard gets his virgins,' remarked Harry. 'No man deserves them more. Well fought blue, red the winner.'

'Agreed, boss,' said Bobby, still looking at the carnage in front, amazed at the destruction the round had wrought. 'Lovely picture it makes sir. Blue sky, mountains in the background, crumbling burnt house with a torched, half naked, battered body hanging from the window sill. The kind that gets the best photograph award.' 'It sure does. It has a certain poignant appeal to it, if captured well. Speaks the tale of Kashmir', said Harry. 'Incidentally Bobby, red is the guy hanging there he is the winner. So don't pat yourself on the back for this round. This bum and his partner deliberately sacrificed themselves to enable the other militants to get away. And I have a nasty suspicion that Mr Khan was around and managed to give us the slip again. Tomorrow I want a full debriefing on the operation. I've decided on some heads in the company that must roll. Three ambush parties run into contact, perfect surprise and what do we finally get? Two militants in the village at the expense of one non fatal. If Prakash hadn't screamed for help and had we stuck to our positions, we would have had a bigger haul. An unsatisfactory operation overall, Bobby.'

A Spring of Surprises
(1400 hrs) | (Dhani Bhaik-2580 mtr)

Money can buy a dog, but not the wag of its tail.

—Tibetan Saying

Sher Khan had stripped his weapon and after cleaning the running parts, was assembling the rifle. He looked at Sahira sitting in the corner, her concentration focused on the roti she was flipping on the fire. In the flickering light, he noticed the dark circles under her eyes and the loss of colour on her pinched face. He realised she had not smiled in a long time and the strain of the life she was leading was tiring her out. The constant move from village to village and hideout to hideout, had drained her utterly and she seemed to have gone beyond caring. He recalled how she was when they had first met. He had been taken by her beauty and courage. She had lovely skin and an easy smile. It had taken courage to have stood in front of that soldier with a loaded rifle. She could easily have been shot. The Sahira he saw now, had visibly aged. He wondered if she loved him.

Since the debacle at Shumrial, Sher Khan was uncertain about his future for the first time. He knew Javed Jabbar had a hand to play in leading the army to Shumrial and cursed himself for underestimating Javed. The sly barber was going to be a far more dangerous threat than the army. He regretted not having eliminated him when he had the chance. A wry smile creased his lips as he realised the web he had spun for himself. The major in Kuligam on one side and the barber turned mujahid, on the other, both baying for his blood. He couldn't understand if the major was after him for killing one of his officers, or for Sahira.

Afghanistan, it struck him, had been a much cleaner and a bigger playing field and one just had to deal with killing Russians instead of all this deceitful politics. For the first time, his thoughts turned to home. While his handlers were pressurising him for a spectacular hit, the fight seemed to have gone out of Sher Khan. He wondered if it was because of his growing attachment to Sahira. He didn't want her to get hurt and felt extremely protective towards her. The feeling surprised him. Was it love? She had gone through hell for him and he would make sure she got the best. There was no choice. She would have to accompany him back to Pakistan.

Sahira on the other hand, was emotionally numb and physically drained. She was living one day to the next. Too frightened of telling Sher Khan she wanted to go home, she had often thought about slipping away to Kupwara to live anonymously. But there was no money. From her present location, she was just a five hour walk away from the Kuligam army post, but wasn't sure if Harry was still there. The last time she had seen him in Shumrial was a few months back and she was aware that army units constantly changed location. Sahira was also uncertain about how Harry would react, especially after he had warned her so many times to keep away from the madness engulfing the valley.

She was angry at Sher Khan for reducing her to a fugitive for no fault of her own. The army and the police knew about her disappearance and regularly harassed her father. The old man had been tortured a couple of times and all this weighed heavily on Sahira's mind. Most of her time now was spent wallowing in self pity and in prayers to Allah for salvation.

Sher Khan knew that the situation demanded immediate redress. Javed as a local, was in a position to trace his whereabouts and like the last time, would use the army to do his dirty work. Javed's survival was directly linked to Sher Khan's permanent departure out of the valley or from this world. He decided to call it a day and head home. He knew permission from his handlers to ex-filtrate would never be granted and they would not understand the ground situation. He would be told the usual—keep low, seize movement and change location. Having taken the decision, he had a chat with Malik and a message was sent to Hathkarhi in Sonapindi to fix a time and date for the return into POK. Sher Khan promised him the fee for his service, from his own pocket.

Unbeknownst to Sher Khan, Hathkarhi had already been bought off by Javed who had anticipated that at some stage, Sher Khan would proceed home. The details of the route, time and date were promptly passed on to Javed in Kalaruch. The date was fixed for the third week of April. The barber waited and plotted his next move on how to convince and involve the major at the Kuligam post. The challenge would be to play it in a manner whereby Sher Khan would be eliminated and a part of the scalp money, which the army gave for information, came to him.

Meanwhile, having closed the loop on his departure plans, Sher Khan was back in his element. His mood changed and his naturally malevolent temperament now needed an outlet. He got down to planning a spectacular attack on the Kuligam post—his parting gift for the Jehad in Kashmir, but before that, he would square the account with the sly barber boy. Tiger, one of the subservient battalion commanders in the Lolab, had grown quite close to Malik. He was now summoned for a meeting.

Tiger mentioned that he often spoke to Javed and was still in touch with him from time to time. In fact, after the shooting incident, Tiger had tried his best to convince him to apologise to Sher Khan. He had agreed to mediate a compromise and had even taken a personal guarantee for Javed's safety. Javed, on the other hand, had been in contact with a few Gujjar militants as he was very keen to get his hands on a sniper rifle. He was prepared to pay but unfortunately, very few were in circulation. Tiger was thereby instructed to get in touch with Javed and, having gained his confidence, to lure him into a trap using the sniper rifle as bait.

The Bait in the Trap

What doesn't kill you makes you stronger.

—Nietzsche

JAVED JABBAR WAS barely twenty-four years old, but time had not been very kind, making him look much older. In a lot of ways, he was still a grown up boy with the usual love for women, weapons and war. As a part of the training in Pakistan he had fired a sniper rifle and had immediately fallen in love. It was his dream to possess one. He knew that the Gujjars along the border, who acted as guides and porters, often stashed away the odd consignment of equipment that came across from Pakistan into Kashmir.

Tantra was one of those elusive figures who in the world of the jehadis was known to have collected a huge stockpile of war-like equipment. He had started his career as a porter and graduated to become one of the most successful guides. In the three years that he was in the business of border crossings, he had apparently accumulated enough stock to start a small war. Instead, Tantra started a business and was the local arms dealer.

While ferrying equipment across from Pakistan as a porter, he and his friend would often secretly cache the load and report back the loss on grounds of bad weather, interception by the Indian army or a host of other reasons which the Pakistani authorities had no way of verifying, even if they suspected anything. The border, in the early years of militancy, was fairly porous and the Pakistanis made full use of this, ensuring a steady stream of supply into Indian territory, while the passes remained free of snow during summer. It was the disappearance of vast stock and regular pilferage over the years, that led to Tantra getting the boot from the job.

Over the years, the tales of his huge stock of weapons were embellished and his secret caches were supposedly spread right across the Shamshabari range. The surrendered local militants who operated with the army, often talked about mule caravans loaded with equipment led by Tantra and his friend Bilal, disappearing regularly. Bilal was apparently killed by the army in an ill-fated border crossing, but the locals believed that Tantra had eliminated his best pal.

Needless to say, Tantra was a marked man by both the security forces and the militants and he did the only thing any man in his shoes would have done. He became a shadow, a ghost figure, often heard on the radio but never seen. Tiger and Tantra were from the same village and had been classmates for a brief period while they were at school. They went into the same line of work and stayed in touch off and on. While Tiger belonged to the Harkat, Tantra was a member of the all Gujjar militant group called the Al-Burq.

Tiger now mentioned his connection with Tantra to Javed during one of their radio conversations and agreed to fix a meeting between them. But first, he insisted both the buyer and the seller should talk over the radio. Tantra confirmed possessing the long *bandook* (as Javed called the sniper rifle) and the price, after a bit of haggling, was fixed.

There was a time when Tantra had a huge stock of weapons, but over the years he had sold most of it. The leftovers were weapons like small ladies pistols and detonators which had no market. He had never owned a sniper rifle. Tiger had paid him handsomely for playing along and Tantra was least interested in knowing what his intentions were when he got Javed, dead or alive. As far as he was concerned, the betrayal did not bother him. After all, both were Kashmiris while he was a Gujjar, and both belonged to different militant groups. If it came down to choosing, then his loyalty was clearly with his old school mate.

Sher Khan and Tiger were sitting in Dharia village drinking tea, when Tantra called on Tiger's radio. The conversation was brief, its purport clear.

'Hello Tiger, *asalaam-walekum*, all okay. The bird will be at Bukhari point just before sundown. *Khuda hafiz*.'

Tiger looked at Sher Khan and smiled. '*Jenab*, your man has taken the bait, and he will be arriving at Bukhari point which is an hour's walk from here in Urni Nar. There is an old, dilapidated *bhaik*, which used to be the point, where in the old days the local launch commander received the infiltrating group of brothers. Imtiaz should be here anytime, so that makes the three of us for the reception party.'

'Don't worry,' answered Sher Khan, patting Tiger's back. 'You don't need so many tigers to kill a jackal. You have done well, brother, and when I meet our seniors across, I shall speak highly of you. Now to make sure we are in ambush to receive the great mujahid and if possible I want him alive.'

Javed Jabbar had a long walk from Kalaruch to Bukhari point and at an easy pace, it had taken him nearly five hours. After collecting the weapon, he planned to spend the night at his sister's house in Tenkpur village. He had an early lunch and had left around mid-day, quite excited at the prospect of his new toy. In a happy mood, with a stick in one hand and singing an old Kashmiri song, Javed Jabbar was quite oblivious to the danger that lurked ahead. He saw the dilapidated hut below, paused and lit a cigarette and then tossing his stick away, and had barely taken a step when a single shot rang out.

Reflexively he threw himself off the path before more rifles joined the song of death. The jungle was thick and fresh undergrowth had filled up the space between the trees providing sufficient cover. Javed knew instantly that he had been tricked and had walked into a trap. He ran blindly sideways and just when he thought he was out of danger, a freak bullet hit his ankle, breaking the bone into pieces. Javed hobbled, swayed and crashed headlong into the bushes, which swallowed him up. He had fallen into a shallow pool, the mouth of which was covered by bushes. Javed heard voices below and recognised Sher Khan's voice berating someone. Before he passed out, Javed had the sense to switch off his radio set and then the world around him went blank.

Sher Khan, Imtiaz and Tiger had made themselves comfortable in the hut with one man keeping watch on the path. Imtiaz had not been told about the plan, and all he knew was they were waiting for someone. He was on sentry duty when he saw Javed coming down the path. He knew immediately what was afoot. If it came to choosing between his Kashmiri brother and a foreign fighter, his loyalties were clearly on the side of his brothers. He was not going to be part of this treachery. Calling for Sher Khan's attention loudly, he let off a single warning shot. He saw Javed roll to the side, get up and run and both Tiger and Sher Khan opened fire on him. Just when Javed seemed to be getting out of range, from the corner of his eye, Imtiaz saw Javed buckle and disappear out of sight.

For the next hour while they searched the area, Sher Khan kept blaming Imtiaz for deliberately alerting Javed. Tiger tried to defend him by calling it accidental fire, but Sher Khan was clear that it had been on purpose. The other two had not seen Javed getting hit and Imtiaz made sure they never went close to where he had last disappeared from sight. The search was aborted and the three of them returned back with Sher Khan in a sullen mood, his faith in the Kashmiris further eroded.

The Pan or the Fire
(2000 HRS)

You Only Live Twice.

—James Bond

WHEN JAVED OPENED his eyes it was pitch dark. He guessed it must be around eight in the night, which meant he had been unconscious for the last three hours or so. He felt a throbbing pain in his right leg and a quick check confirmed the bullet had smashed his ankle bone. He knew that if he didn't get medical attention soon, he would die. Clenching his teeth and summoning great will power, Javed managed to pull himself erect on his one good foot and began the painful ordeal to find help. A motorable jungle track, built by the forest department for transporting timber, ran barely an hour from where he now stood. But it took him another three hours to go down cross-country before he dragged himself and flopped down on the road, completely spent. His clothes torn, body lacerated and bruised, Javed Jabbar was as close to death by exhaustion as a man can be. The will to survive however, still flickered strong in the ex-barber.

But luck seemed to be on his side. A short while later, a forest department truck collecting timber came down on its way to

Kuligam, where the department had their depot. In the headlight, the driver saw a badly wounded man lying prone across the track and his first thoughts were that the person had perhaps been mauled by a leopard. The man was conscious and the driver and his partner carried him down to a couple of unused shepherd huts. They made him comfortable, covered him with a shawl, bandaged his foot crudely with a handkerchief, lit a fire in the corner and propped his weapon next to him. The man then asked them to go down to Varno village to fetch a doctor.

At two in the morning, Major Hari Haran, company commander Kuligam post, was woken up from his sleep by the sentry on duty. The frightened driver and his partner were ushered in.

'A wounded mujahid, you say?' asked a still sleepy Harry. 'Strange. We've had no contact and no other army unit could be operating in our area. Are you certain it was a gunshot wound?'

'*Jenab*, he has a gun and is in bad shape,' said the driver. 'He can't possibly walk. He is waiting for us to get him the doctor. We have told you the place sir, can we go home now?'

'No you can't,' said Harry. 'Well done, but the job is only half complete. He is waiting for the doctor and the doctor will arrive in your truck. To walk will take another two hours.' 'Sahib,' Harry addressed the *subedar* standing in the corner, 'give them a cup of tea and get ten men ready. Unload the timber from the truck and tell Bobby sahib to rise and shine. Departure in the next twenty minutes.'

From the dispensary at Khurama, the road swings north along the riverbed and turns into a potholed dirt track. In forty minutes, they arrived at the stream crossing and eight men got off with orders to walk up the stream and cover the huts from the south. Bobby and Harry continued in the truck. The driver was instructed to keep the engine running and the two of them walked down towards a hut where a fire could be seen flickering through the cracks in the wooden wall. Both the officers were wearing shalwar kameez and *phiran*s.

Lady luck, it seemed, had deserted Javed once again and was intent on playing a cruel game of Lolab roulette. He was lying with his head resting on a log next to the fire, dozing in and out of sleep, when he heard the truck. His hopes went up and he thanked Allah. In his weakened state he saw two men enter with weapons. While one of them kicked his rifle away, the other scooped him up and turned him around. In a jiffy, his hands were tied behind his back. It had happened so fast that he was not even sure whether it was real or if he was hallucinating in his current condition.

He saw the two strangers looking down at him with an amused but bored sort of expression. Javed's first thought was they were Sher Khan's men, but then the tall one with the beard spoke and Javed's innards shrank, for he had heard the voice many times on the radio and knew immediately that it belonged to the major at Kuligam. It was the army this time.

'*Asalaam-walekum*,' said Harry. 'You asked for a doctor and we got here as soon as possible.' There was a brief pause. 'From an initial inspection, your state is not good, but don't worry. As a doctor, let me tell you,' and he looked deeply into Javed's eyes, 'it's going to get worse, brother.'

And at that, both men laughed. 'Treating a mujahidin,' he continued, 'is like mind over matter. I don't mind and you don't matter.' More laughter followed.

The two were clearly enjoying themselves and from their behaviour, Javed knew he could expect no mercy. His course was run and his time drawing near. The only hope was to somehow manage a swift death. He definitely could stand no more pain. Something told him that to lie and beg for clemency would be useless.

'Right,' said the tall man, making himself comfortable next to the fire while the other stood leaning against the wall. 'We are all honourable people in this hut and call ourselves soldier. Soldiers of Allah or soldiers of a nation, but soldiers all the same. So let's speak the truth. Any deviation from the truth and I will know and it shall fetch you exquisite pain.'

Harry picked up a burning twig from the fire and lit Javed's long beard. There was a spark, a sizzle, and a simmering glow appeared at the end of his fast diminishing beard. The embers extinguished before they could reach his chin, and an acrid smell of burnt hair filled the small hut.

'Start with your name and bring us up to date of how you happen to have presented yourself to us on a platter.'

Javed paused for some time to collect his thoughts and then gave out his name. There was a moment of silence as both the officers exchanged a look and Bobby viciously kicked his broken ankle.

'The barber, or someone with a similar name?' he asked, as Javed winced in pain and tried to move his injured leg out of Bobby's reach.

'The barber, *jenab*.'

'Talk about luck! Look at him—with his bloody reputation, one would expect a larger than life figure and what do we have here! With this kind of a build you should have stuck to cutting hair!' exclaimed Harry, examining the razor they had found in his pocket. 'You still like carrying the tools of your last profession don't you? Really Javed, minus your weapon you are such a nice man that we can actually have a decent conversation now.

So how long have you been a militant or a mujahid, whichever is politically correct, depending on which side of the fence one stands?'

'*Hazoor*, I should be completing four winters,'

'You see, Bobby?' and Harry switched to English, 'some wise guy has calculated that the average life of an active militant is about four years. This guy is just about there.'

'You bet sir, so he is a good militant then. You hear that Javed, you are good mujahid. *Shabash*!' answered Bobby, patting Javed's dirty matted hair, as one would a dog.

'And a battalion commander in four years,' continued Harry. 'He is a career militant! A pity his innings comes to an end.'

Javed didn't understand the exchange in English between the two officers, but he knew they were talking about him.

'Javed,' said Harry, 'you have done better than me in your profession. I am just a major in eleven years of hard service and look at you, a battalion commander in just four years!'

'But, *jenab*,' Javed tried a bit of servile flattery, 'you are an officer who commands a regular company and highly paid in your job. I am just a small man, who out of necessity had to become a mujahid to earn a little money. If I had the same opportunities that you have had in your life, why would have I followed this path?'

The deep stare that Harry fixed on Javed made him wonder if his appeal had touched a sympathetic chord in the man. But a little later he felt uncomfortable under the gaze, especially with the cruel half smile that lingered more in the eyes than on Harry's lips.

'Javed Jabbar,' Harry finally spoke. 'Given better circumstances you would still have been a murderer and a bigger one at that.

The police profile and your reputation amongst the villagers confirm you as a bloody psychopath. Why do you still carry a razor, friend?'

'On happy days,' interjected Bobby, 'he probably gives his mates a shave to stay in practice. Maybe he plans to run an upmarket salon, when all this jehad nonsense is over.' Both the officers chuckled.

They sat in silence except for the odd question to verify facts, while Javed narrated the story up until his arrival in the hut.

'The rest you know, sir,' he continued, 'I was in any case going to pass on information about Sher Khan's departure to you. The third week of this month, between the fifteenth to the eighteenth, has moonless nights and the attempt to cross will be during that time. They plan to use the Rang route. Bagalsor to Palpathri, leaving Kanzalwan and Bagtor to the right. Then they will hit the Naushera nar and cross over into POK. A Gujjar by the name of Hathkari is the guide and I have paid him to lead the group till Palpathri. He will make sure they arrive at night and thereafter he will desert. Sher Khan is yours for the taking.'

'And how can we trust you? Who knows, you may be leading us into a trap.' Bobby piped up.

'*Jenab*, if your firing standards had been better in Shumrial, you would have practically wiped out militancy in the Lolab,' he answered sarcastically. 'There were nearly twenty mujahids in the village that day and five or six were senior commanders including Sher Khan. Incidentally, that information was provided by me.'

'How many in the group?' asked Bobby

'I don't know…Three or four maybe. Hathkari might take a young lad along, who he is training as a guide. I could take you till Palpathri—I have a score to settle with Sher Khan.'

'No thanks,' said Bobby. 'You are like a blind grenade, completely unpredictable, and who the hell will keep an eye on you all along? In any case, every Gujjar and his dog in north Lolab, knows the way to Palpathri.'

'Are we carrying any tea Bobby? Just tell someone to get a cup for him too and something to eat.'

Javed's hands were untied and he hauled himself up on one elbow to drink his tea noisily. He devoured a handful of glucose biscuits, the crumbs littering his half burnt beard as the two men sat quietly and watched the last human actions of a dead man. It's always sad to watch life extinguished, especially human and if the condemned man conducts himself with dignity, it does lend a certain poignant grace to the setting.

'Right,' Harry spoke, as Javed finished the last drags of his tea. 'Are you a good Muslim, the kind who prays five times a day?'

Javed nodded, uncertain about where the line of questioning was leading.

'Then tell me honestly, what you would have done, if you had me in a similar situation. And be honest, for unlike what you see in the movies, nothing that you say will be held against you in the court of law. This is the court and I am the judge and the jury and the verdict…Well, it has already been decided.'

Javed could feel the shadow of death very near. He had fought hard to live. Tired and in pain, he now gave up. He knew he had to bow to the will of Allah some time, and if one had to go, then one might as well speak the truth and go in style.

'*Jenab*,' answered Javed without hesitation, 'You see the razor in your hand? I would have used it to slit your throat.'

'Glad you spoke the truth, Javed, 'replied Harry, showing no surprise. 'If you had lied and told me anything else, I had decided to test the razor and instead of the *kalma*, I would have recited the *gayatri mantra*[1]. That would have had you kicked out of *jannat* for sure. But I will keep my promise and be merciful. You have five minutes to say your namaz.'

'I had already recited my *kalma* when you caught me. I am ready, *jenab*.'

Harry, looking at the man, couldn't but marvel at his composure in the face of death. He wondered if he would have acquitted himself in a similar fashion. What was going on in the man's head?

'Javed, do you have any regret about turning a militant, now that you are about to die? If you had followed a more peaceful path, maybe you would have been married with kids. There must be some remorse at this early death.'

'None,' answered Javed, looking Harry straight in the eye. 'It was Allah's desire that I become a mujahid and it was written that I die at your hand. The woman who could have been the mother of my children is already with Allah.'

'Get up then and sit in a kneeling position, facing the corner.'

'You shoot a mujahid in the front and not in the back, jenab,' answered Javed.

'Can't but admire your style. For a *hajam*[2], you make a good militant. Pity you are fighting on the wrong side,' said Harry, kneeling in front of him. 'Any messages for any one?' In a whisper, he asked about the Gujjar woman with Sher Khan.

'She is his woman, *jenab* and plans to cross over into Pakistan with him. Promise me you will get Sher Khan for what he did to me and have no pity. Kill that bitch too.'

---

[1] A rhyme from *Rig Veda*.
[2] Barber.

The nine millimetre Beretta bullet fired at point blank range, made a neat hole in the forehead and splattered his brains on the soot blackened wall behind. Strangely, Javed didn't collapse immediately but shuddered a few times, before keeling over, his head hitting the fire with a thud. Blood and brains sizzled and roasted and the smell of burning flesh and hair filled the cabin. Both the officers with expressionless faces looked on for some time, and then, tossing the razor into the fire, the two walked out.

Kuligam Army Post
(1500 HRS)

Tout casse, tout passé, tout lasse.
'Everything passes, perishes and palls.'
—French proverb

THERE WAS FEVERISH activity in camp before the patrol set out. This was not going to be one of the usual operations in and around the Lolab Basin, as it was way out in the back of beyond of wilderness. Harry anticipated that the operation might continue for five to six days and therefore preparations had to be made accordingly. At times, they would be touching more than three thousand metres and the snow had yet to melt completely. In fact, if the weather packed up, there were strong chances of rain and snow at that height. One had to think about casualty evacuation too, for there could be a possibility that a chopper might not be available or may not be able to land.

As Javed had given no exact date, Harry wanted to be on the safe side by turning up a day or two early, around Palpathri. The two officers sat outside on the steps of the cottage and watched Balwinder, Harry's buddy, pack their rucksacks for the trip. Bobby looked on wistfully as the rucksack grew in size and weight. Finally, as the last extra magazine was being shoved in, he cracked.

'Hold it, Bally,' and he got up and picked up the sack, and with a resentful sigh, he turned on Harry. 'Hey Boss, how do you expect us to fight after lugging all this weight up the mountain. This must be more than thirty kilos, and if an officer is carrying so much, I can quite imagine that some of the men, the RL guys, will have easily five to seven kilos more. It's a fighting patrol, not an expedition.'

'You know the old saying,' answered Harry, with a smile. 'Climb slow, descend fast and fight easy. The extra ammo is tipping the balance and I am not reducing it one bit. You run into a big group and you have a fight on your hand, and there is no cavalry arriving to bail you out at that height. What if some of Sher Khan's pals have decided to see him off?'

Bobby kept quiet, picking up the sack a few times to convince himself.

'Well then can we reduce the height? Why do we have to go so far up the mountain, when the path is clearly much lower?'

'For the simple reason that mountain warfare is about height domination,' answered Harry, a trifle irritated. 'If there is to be a contact, then I prefer fighting top down. And you know from experience. Remember Hafruda. Bloody five guys had pinned us down and if it hadn't been for the darkness, we would never have been able to extract Rajbir. For a little extra weight and few metres more, I am not risking lives.'

Two days later they had set out and Harry now called for a halt, as he leaned his heavy rucksack against a tree. He felt immediate relief as the weight came off, easing the flow of blood to his strained shoulders. He looked down and saw men flopping on either side of the narrow track, each trying to find the most comfortable position to ease the burden on his back. The sixty degree gradient and the unusually heavy loads, were taking a toll. Maybe Bobby was right and the load too much. They still had another fifteen hours to climb and most of it in the darkness. Some of the guys were so heavily weighed, they had to be helped to stand.

The plan was to reach Bagalsor by morning, split the party, each under the command of the two officers and encircle Palpathri. Thereafter, they had to sit tight and keep the target under surveillance, till Sher Khan and party were sighted. The ground situation would decide the future course of action once contact was made with the militants.

Harry was unsure about what he would do with Sahira. There were mixed feelings for her after Javed had told him about her leaving with Sher Khan. A part of him was still attracted to her, but to leave her kith and kin and her country for a militant, confirmed a great love she had for him. He felt cheated and betrayed a second time by a woman. His mind was a whirlpool of emotions. Was it love? Why did he expected any loyalty from her? After all, he had never ever promised her anything. Was it just a crush, which he, like a teenager, was confusing for love? Or was it a purely physical attraction, often a stronger emotion in the short run than love?

His ego was hurt. Hurt that he had spent time in her house so often, given her the odd gift and in spite of all his advice, she had still strayed off the path, courting a militant. The last thought evoked a great rage in him. Forget the woman and focus on the job, he chided himself as he climbed. They hit Bagalsor at three thousand metres, just as the day was breaking. It was an undulating pasture the size of a football field with a few unoccupied shepherd huts. The Gujjars and their cattle would start arriving by the end of the month and become the source of sustenance for the numerous bands of mujahidin, drifting in and across the porous border.

Ishaq, the local guide with them, pointed out the various landmarks. They could see Palpathri further up the mountain—a small flat land on a spur, with the usual huts. Leaving a few men at Bagalsor, the column split, to climb higher, traverse the mountain and come up on either side of Palpathri. The place would be under observation, the distance rendering it impossible to dominate by fire. However, both parties on either side had the height advantage to close in, in a pincer movement, in case Sher Khan decided to flee further up the mountain. Harry looked up to see the sun touching the peaks, the higher slopes of which were still snow bound. In fact, there was still snow in patches, under trees and in the nalas and gullies. Like a good mountaineer, he was in the habit of constantly looking at the sky to read the weather and a dark patch of cloud in the south-east looked ominous enough to bother him. If the weather packed up and visibility fell, the whole operation could be in jeopardy.

He adjusted the straps of the rucksack, shifted the rifle from his right to the other shoulder and plodded upwards, imagining a scene where a dead Sher Khan was presented to Sahira and how he would gloat, seeing her expression. He recalled lines from a poem by Tennyson that would be appropriate for such an occasion;

Home they bought her warrior dead.
She neither swooned nor uttered cry.
All her maidens watching said,
She must weep or she will die.

Dhani Bhaik
(1700 HRS)

Tell zeal it wants devotion;
Tell love it is but lust;
Tell time it is but motion;
Tell flesh it is but dust;
And wish them not reply;
For thou must give the lie.

—Sir Walter Raleigh

HATHKARI WAS ESCORTED by Malik into the log hut. Sher Khan, sitting next to the fire, got up to greet him. He got the impression that Sher Khan was extremely effusive in his welcome. He shook his hand for a long time and then put an affectionate arm around Hathkari's shoulder. He thought that Sher Khan probably had respect for someone who was the best in the trade, or possibly more because his own survival now depended on Hathkari's expertise to get him back home.

Hathkari remembered the face. It had been about a year since they had crossed paths. The man had lost weight, and grey hair was visible in his beard and long hair. But it was the eyes that succinctly gave out the story of his year-long stay in

Kashmir—they looked hunted. He remembered Sher Khan well, for he had been told by the major to take extra care and make sure he got across into India safely. He cast a quick look at Sahira sitting sulkily in the corner, and knew immediately that they were a couple.

She looked equally jaded. He got the impression that they had been fighting. Probably doesn't want him to leave, he guessed. None of his business, he was making a fair amount of money from this deal. He had taken ten thousand plus an AK-47 from Javed and another ten thousand from Sher Khan as an advance. Twenty thousand and a weapon for just a walk and no risk, was the best deal he had ever made. He also sensed Malik's dislike for the woman.

'*Jenab*,' said Hathkari, sipping tea, 'I hope we are all set to move tonight, only three days of darkness left. I had a boy coming along but he is not well and has dropped out. Is it just the two of you, or are any more mujahids expected?'

'Three. Malik, self and the woman comes along too,' answered Sher Khan.

Hathkari looked surprised and exchanged a quick glance with Malik, who averted his gaze and looked down, his disapproval of the idea quite clear.

'Well,' answered Hathkari, clearing his throat in hesitation, 'in the old days I have taken families across with kids, but those days are over. The border is tightly sealed and crossing is a highly risky venture, besides being physically demanding. With a woman in tow, your exposure increases and she will slow you down. You are highly vulnerable in case you have a contact with the army.'

'The price is increased. My weapon is yours on the other side, but the woman comes with us.'

Sitting in the corner listening, Sahira's hopes were that she would be allowed to stay back, but Sher Khan dashed them instantly and Hathkari put up no further resistance. Well he didn't want to. After all, he had no intention of crossing the border.

Sahira was briefly tempted to tell them that she might be pregnant, but knew it would only harden Sher Khan's resolve to take her across. In the past few days, she had been feeling nauseous and had finally gone across to the local mid-wife for a chat. The symptoms confirmed that she was pregnant. She had decided not to share the news with Sher Khan for fear he would insist on her going back with him. Whatever feelings she had once felt for him were dead and she was miserable carrying the child of a man she now nearly detested. On the other hand, she noticed he had mellowed a little towards her lately, as if making up for all the punishment he was subjecting her to. It will all be over, he kept telling her. This is the last jehad for me.

Within four hours of the climb, Sahira was utterly spent, taking regular breaks, guzzling water and irritating Hathkari and Malik. The delay cost them reaching Bagtor by morning. Hathkari called for a halt in a thicket next to a stream. He pulled out thick corn rotis and some sabzi and everybody had a bite before getting some shut-eye. Daylight travel had been forbidden by Hathkari and the altered plan was to depart around six in the evening, bypass Bagtor, climb for barely an hour and hit Palpathri by eleven in the night. Unbeknownst to them however, the delay had been a divine intervention. As per Hathkari's original plan they were supposed to have spent the day at Bagtor in one of the empty huts and would surely have clashed with the five men from Harry's team occupying the place.

The next climb however, was not that taxing and by ten that night, they were in one of the huts at Palpathri. The weather had turned cold and the little starlight they had the previous night, was all but gone, hidden behind dark clouds. The temptation to light a fire was strong, but Hathkari was very strict about it. On the pretext of reconnoitring the area for the next day's march, Hathkari, after having some food and promising to be back in fifteen minutes, departed. That was the last time anybody in the group ever saw him. Within minutes of his stepping out of the hut, the swirling mist rolling up the valley had swallowed him and Hathkari bounded down the familiar path, on his way to Bagtor. He reckoned that by morning he would be back in his village in Sonapindi for a hot cup of tea.

Sher Khan had learnt his lessons and learnt them the hard way. His trust in the locals had taken a hard knock. Within ten minutes of Hathkari's disappearance, he knew something was amiss. He called Malik to get ready and roughly hauled Sahira up on her feet. She swayed a little and then lay back on the ground. Sher Khan hauled her up again, whispering encouragement and instructing Malik at the same time.

'We have been betrayed, I think,' he said. 'It's the barber, I am sure. May he rot in *jahanum*. Switch on your radio and stay close. There is very little time to lose. If it comes to a fight, brother, the two of us are equal to five local mujahids and this time the barber's corpse will go down the mountain. We need to get height and then swing westwards towards the border.'

'Leave the woman. She is no state to move and in any case it's her people—they will take her back.'

'No,' snapped Sher Khan, helping Sahira out of the hut, 'I know Javed and his hatred for me will come out on her. I can't leave her at Javed's mercy.'

Hathkari in the meanwhile, passed the pond at a fast clip, heading towards the dead tree which he knew was exactly three minutes away and from where the path veered left towards Bagtor. He hit the tree and was quite pleased with his memory for detail. He remembered a large rock a few steps ahead of the tree and just to reinforce his view he briefly stopped and peered in the mist. He saw the dark silhouette of the rock and smiled—not bad for someone coming after seven months and that too in darkness and poor visibility! It struck him that he knew his mountains better than he knew the body of his third wife. He felt a stirring between his legs at the thought of her young, warm body. Dreaming of her, he went past the first hut at Bagtor. It was the last thought he would ever carry, for he went no further, as a hail of gunfire from the hut killed him instantly.

Sher Khan was in front, with Sahira in the middle and Malik bringing up the rear. They had climbed for fifteen minutes when they heard gunshots from below. They paused, trying to figure out what was happening, when suddenly Malik's radio locked onto an unidentified station and briefly, they heard a conversation in English. Sher Khan understood enough of the language to figure out that they were talking about the current situation and that it was the army. In fact, he thought one of voices sounded rather familiar, but he could not place where he had heard it before.

'The officer from Kuligam,' said Malik from behind. 'Sheru bhai, the guide was bought off by the barber and the dog then tips off the army or probably works for them. It's an elaborate trap and we paid for it!'

Sahira had also recognised the voice and now, she suddenly felt better. There was hope that Harry would save her. She must give some indication of her presence, or at least try and ensure he didn't lose their trail. In the darkness, she broke some bangles and dropped them on the ground.

Sher Khan was perplexed by Harry. For the first time, he felt admiration for the man. The guy had the drive and the ability to turn up at the most unexpected of places. And he could take punishment like a good mujahid, and probably was one in his last birth. Pity there would be no chance to fight, for he planned to climb as high as possible before turning west. It was just a matter of lasting longer in the wilderness and the army would crack. He set a blistering pace.

Bobby came on the line breaking radio silence.

'Girwar has shot a local militant, Hotel-One, probably the guide heading back after depositing the goods at Papa.'

'We have lost surprise and my guess, Sierra Kilo is going to break out. Without a guide, he will climb and hit the ridgeline going west, roger so far? Bravo-Two, proceed to Palpathri, cordon the place and sit tight. I don't want a firefight in the darkness. First light, conduct a search and start climbing, for I think the birds have already flown. I am moving up with a small party over.'

'Wilco over,' replied Bobby.

Harry selected five of the fittest men, all with seven to ten years of hard soldiering in their early thirties. They reduced the weight, but carried extra ammo. Harry checked his watch and the luminous dial showed just over one in the morning. Visibility was getting worse, with the temperature falling and threatening snow. As a marathon runner and a high altitude climber, he thought, if I can't beat this group to the top, then I deserve to play bloody marbles for the rest of my life. Briefly he thought of Sahira and hoped that she hadn't come along or had been left behind in the huts at Palpathri.

For an hour Sahira kept up with Sher Khan and then she started to drop back. Malik now led the way and Sher Khan dragged, cajoled and bullied her to continue. Just shy of daybreak and six hundred meters below the ridgeline, she finally gave up. It was meant to be a short break, but she just lay down and went off to sleep. No amount of shaking could make her open her eyes, or move her limbs. For the time being, she was beyond recovery. Sher Khan looked at her and realised he had to give her some rest. They had been on the move with just a few hours sleep after the first days climb, with little food and in bad weather, for the past thirty-six hours. His own injured arm was giving him hell.

'A little more and we should hit the ridge,' he addressed Malik, 'I remember it's just a flat walk till we go down to the river thereafter. Try and call Mushtaq bhai across and request for help. We need a local guide or else we run the risk of running into the army. I hope his radio's switched on'.

Malik climbed a little higher and selected an open patch. He started calling Mike Charlie, the controller in Pakistan. Within a few attempts, a familiar voice answered.

'*Asalaam-walekum*, Malik, all okay?'

A huge relief surged through Malik, just to hear that voice. He could almost feel as though he was home. MC would manage something.

'*Walekum salaam*[1], *jenab*,' answered Malik, 'I'm afraid things are not alright. Wait, speak to someone,' and he came down and handed the set to Sher Khan.

'What are you doing here, much out of your area of operation?' he questioned. 'Why was no one informed about this move? Go back to Lolab and we'll fix the right way to do this.'

'Can't go back,' answered Sher Khan. 'Look, we are in deep trouble, the army is pursuing us. We have reached so far, and all we ask is

[1] And peace be upon you, response to *Asalaam-walekum*.

a local man to guide us the last few kilometres. Our location is Bird Peak, tell the man who comes in to speak to me and I will direct him to our position. I will give all the explanations for this sudden departure to you in person. Everybody is listening to this conversation, so please hurry.'

And everybody was listening. The militant chatter had been picked up by the army unit deployed at the border. An excited Sonny Nambiar was sitting in the battalion headquarter mess reading a two-week old newspaper. The evening before, he had come down from his post and was on his way to a spot of hard earned leave. He was excited because his ex-girl friend had hinted that she was bored with the computer salesman and Namby was hopeful they might get together again. Patience, he told himself. Five more days to go.

Major Kohli, the Adjutant, walked in and ordered a coffee. Pulling up a chair he sat very solemnly in front of Namby.

'Come on, sir,' said Namby. 'Give it to me straight—leave cancelled again. I haven't had a day off in a year.'

'No, it's not that bad, kid. Postponed would be the right word. There is a lot of militant chatter we are picking up and the direction finder shows it coming from somewhere around the mouth of Naushera Nar. Quite close to the ridgeline. It's an ex-filtrating group and they seem to have lost their way. They are flapping about like mad, asking all and sundry for help. The CO wants you to take his Quick Reaction Team (QRT) and walk up the Nar towards the peak. They are sitting ducks but caution, the buggers are cornered and will put up resistance. The sooner you wrap this, the sooner you can be on your way home.

Sher Khan decided to wait until MC could organise a guide, instead of aimlessly wandering about. The forest had thinned out, as they were at the periphery of the tree line. In the arbor of a few shunted trees, Sher Khan called for a break and decided to catch a little sleep himself. He had barely gone to sleep when he was roused roughly by Malik who was on guard.

'They are here,' he said, pointing downhill towards an exposed stretch of the path. 'About half a kilometre away.'

'Who, the guides?' answered Sher Khan, a little dazed.

'No Sheru bhai, the army. I doubt there is any guide coming to fetch us. We might as well make a stand and die like true mujahids.'

'Not yet,' answered Sher Khan, rousing Sahira. 'We can still make it, brother. If the army is climbing, I think we should go down, traverse west and climb back later.'

With Sher Khan leading, they went down at a fast clip. Sahira, by now, was completely oblivious to her situation. She was like a zombie obeying orders. The little food eaten the night before had promptly been thrown up during her morning sickness. At some stage during the climb, she had felt a wet stickiness between her legs and was shocked to discover blood. Silently, she had wept for her un-born child, begging Allah for forgiveness. Neither Sher Khan nor Malik had noticed.

They were on the leeward side of the mountain and the snow had yet to melt completely. The forest was gloomy and quiet and the only sound was the crunch of boots going through hard snow. Sher Khan went down a gully, took a turn and froze like the snow around him—unbelievably, there was another army column coming up the same path! If it hadn't been for the mist, he would have blundered into them. Clutching Sahira by the arm, he turned and went back up the way they had come.

Namby had been walking for the past three hours and was in a foul mood. He had often been sent on these wild goose chases by the signal detachment on some intercept they would pick. Their direction finders were obsolete and gave the general direction with no accurate distance. He was about to call it a day and turn back, when in a shallow gully, he noticed what looked like boot marks in the snow. He sat down and observed the tell tale signs of human presence. There were clearly three or four people in the group and they had retraced their steps. In all probability, they had sighted him and turned. For once, the Signal guys were correct. Something about one of the boot marks looked familiar. Then he recalled the first and the only infiltration that had taken place through his area, around the same month last year. The sole looked a little worn out, but the size was unmistakable. It was definitely the same big bastard. 'See the foot prints?' he told the lead scout. 'Follow it till we meet the owners. It's tracking uphill, so go very slow and deliberate. This is one man I need to square an account with.'

Bobby's radio crackled, 'What's up Bravo-One, I am sitting here getting cold,' Harry's voice came through with a lot of static in the background. 'They seem to have disappeared without a trace.'

'Not really,' answered Bobby. 'Snow White seems to be leaving a trail that a blind man could follow.' But the message was lost as he went down into a nala and communication was severed.

For the first time in his life, Sher Khan nearly gave up. What with fatigue, hunger and the gunshot wound giving him pain, he lost all ability to reason and plan calmly. It was not in his temperament to play this cat and mouse game for so long, especially if he was the mouse, and he was running short on patience now. Mumbling something to himself, he roughly dragged Sahira along, who if left alone would promptly sit down. Malik viewed him with concern and timidly suggested they abandon the girl. But Sher Khan would not hear of it. She had come too far and endured too much to be treated like that. In any case, it was not his style to abandon the people who were close to him, and especially not a woman he loved.

When they had been climbing for a few hours, Sher Khan called for a halt. They sat down behind some rocks and Sahira, as had become her habit, stretched out and went off to sleep. Sher Khan looked at his watch and felt hopeful about having shaken off the pursuit. Another couple of hours and darkness would be their friend. Both he and Malik put their weapons down, and facing what they thought was west, went down on their knees to offer namaz. But they never got a chance to complete it. Having made his obeisance twice, as Sher Khan came up, from the corner of his eyes, he noticed movement a hundred yards to the left. He pulled Malik down and the next time, peered over the rock, where the trees in front seemed to be full of men. They exchanged a look, which needed no words, silently picked up their weapons and taking cover, opened fire.

Harry, having waited for a few hours on the ridge, decided to climb down and sweep towards the Naushera Nar. Maybe the militants never made it to the top, guessing that the army may already be waiting on the heights, he thought. If they hadn't run into Bobby climbing up, then maybe they had swung west somewhere short of the ridge, and were planning to hit the Nar using the more difficult route. Harry arrived at an open patch with a couple of large rocks in the middle and a half constructed mud platform for a hut on one side, which the builder never really got down to completing.

The Gujjar guide stopped, pointed at something across the clearing and got into a huddle with the scouts. Harry joined them and standing behind a thick deodar tree, they discussed what it could be. On a stark branch of a small bush, a tiny swatch of red cloth fluttered in the breeze like a prayer flag and the snow around it looked trampled. The scouts didn't think much about it, but the Gujjar was suspicious and held Harry back from stepping out into the clearing. It wasn't a long discussion, as the answer came in the form of a burst of gunfire from the rocks in front. God, it had taken nearly forty-five hours of hard labour to get the contact, thought Harry and this was not counting the additional twenty-four hours they had spent arriving early.

'Spread out and engage!' he shouted. 'And no bravado, there are still two hours of daylight left and Gurung keep calling Bravo-Two till you make contact.'

The firefight was sharp and controlled. It was a fight between well trained professional fighters on both sides. Unlike the movies, there were no long bursts of automatic fire from the hip. They traded aimed, single shots to preserve ammunition. Sahira woke up with a start to loud gunfire at her elbow. For a second she didn't know where she was and then it struck her, and instinctively in panic, she tried to get up to run. Sher Khan pulled her down.

'Keep your head down,' he snarled into her face. 'Malik, you see the broken tree? Left of it is your arc of responsibility. I'll take care of the right.'

Below on the mountain, Namby was making slow progress. The boot marks would often disappear, where the snow had melted and it was time consuming to regain the trail. One had to be extremely careful of walking into an ambush. The trail went cold again and Namby indicated to the points men to check the area to his left. They were still searching, when gunfire was heard from further up to the right of their location. Namby contacted base and the Adjutant came on the line.

'Alpha-One, there is gunfire somewhere ahead over.'

If Major Kohli hated anything, it was decisions and questions and Namby was perpetually badgering him with the two.

'Are you informing me or asking me, Namby?' he asked irritatedly. 'You are the man on ground.'

'Informing sir,' answered Namby. 'Are there any other army units operating? I don't want a blue on blue situation.'

'Hey General, I would have told you if I had that information, right. Maybe they are fighting amongst themselves.'

'Perhaps you are right sir,' said Namby, affronted with the way Kohli had spoken. 'Perhaps they disagreed about the path they ought to take and decided to settle it with a duel. Over and out Sir.'

The firefight had been going on for half an hour and Harry was concerned about the impending darkness. Another hour and the odds would increasingly tip in favour of the opposition. Where was Bobby? There was no radio contact and the only hope was that he had heard the firing and was making his way towards it. There was a desperate need for more troops to tighten the cordon.

Malik crawled up to Sher Khan for there was barely a metre of cover behind the rocks.

'Sheru bhai,' he spoke in his ears, loud enough to be heard above the din of gun fire. 'Let the girl go, she doesn't deserve to die. They will take her surrender.'

Sher Khan looked at the scared, prostrate figure of the girl and relented. Sometimes, one must let go of the most precious of possessions. He had completely forgotten about her in the heat of battle. He placed a hand on her back and felt her body trembling. He wondered if it was fright or whether she was crying. He had spent all his life with strong men and couldn't understand weakness in the face of death. Tearing a part of her shalwar he tied it to the barrel of his rifle and raised it. The firing from across stopped.

'*Fauji* bhai,' he shouted keeping his head down. 'The girl is innocent, and she is coming out. Don't fire.' He ran his fingers through her hair, patted her head affectionately and nudged her to stand. He could see she was struggling to tell him something, but finding it difficult to talk. She was clearly scared, he thought. He went closer and made out the word 'child'. It made no sense to Sher Khan.

'Forgive me if you can and may Allah be with you,' he whispered in her ear, as she stood up, hesitating and mustering the courage to walk forward.

Harry looked at her and couldn't believe what forty plus hours of being hunted in the mountains could do to a hardy young woman. Her shalwar was torn and covered with mud and her hair was dishevelled and fell in untidy knots over her face. In the mist, from a distance she looked like some ghost figure from a cheap, B-grade horror movie. Watching her standing there dazed, it made Harry wonder if she might be drugged. Quite a few of the militants were on opium. Sahira stood still, unsure which way to walk or perhaps she was too frightened. While all eyes were on her, Malik tugged Sher Khan's sleeves.

'Time to go Sheru bhai,' he said. 'I am going to make it to the tree and then cover you. They won't fire, the girl's in the way. *Khuda hafiz.*'

It was again the Gujjar who sighted Malik at the other end of the rocks, directly behind Sahira. It wasn't very clear, but someone was trying to crawl away and reach the trees. He pointed it out to Harry. There was no time to waste, any minute now the man would reach the trees and escape. Harry picked up his rifle and found Sahira looming large in his sights. He tried to aim from either side of her but just couldn't get a clear shot. He shouted for her to sit down or move aside, but she seemed to be paralysed and showed no sign of acknowledging his command. None of the soldiers fired, knowing Harry's strict instruction in dealing with kids, animals and women. 'They were to be treated with kindness and respect,' he would often tell them, 'and in that order of priority.' The havildar behind spat loudly and abused.

'Come on, sahib,' he said flustered. 'Not a second time, with the same woman helping them to get away again, especially the man who killed Ash sahib. Why did we make all this effort? Give me the order if you are hesitating.'

Harry heard the remark and it struck him that it had been Havildar Saifullah Khan who had exhorted him to fire on the fateful day that Sahira had stood in front of Sher Khan, nearly a year ago. It enraged Harry to see how she protected Sher Khan all the time. So many people had died because of that one folly on his part and the woman was taking advantage of his weakness for her. He heard Saifullah Khan lower his rifle with a huge sigh of frustration and Harry pressed the trigger. Sahira was thrown back disappearing behind the rocks. Malik however, had reached the trees and now, taking cover, he opened fire. Harry could hear Malik beseeching Sher Khan to make the break and he waited to get a clear shot if he did so. But Sher Khan was not going anywhere, now or ever.

He crouched behind a rock, laid out his ammo pouch, tore and ate up the code page, smashed his radio set on the rock and the watch presented by his pal Omar in Afghanistan and muttering a *kalma* prepared for death. Briefly, the thought crossed Malik's mind that he ought to go back, but before he could make the dash, Sher Khan waved for him to go. The last Malik would recall of his friend in later years, was Sher Khan crouching next to the bullet riddled body of the woman, his hand on his chest—a gesture of farewell. Then Malik ran uphill as fast as he could, the thick forest protecting him from all the fire directed at him.

It was an ill matched fight and the volume of fire brought upon Sher Khan rendered him incapable of firing back. Within ten minutes, he had received multiple gunshots in both his arms and his shoulder. A bullet grazed his cheek and Sher Khan fell back, unconscious and bleeding profusely. Harry waited for a while before walking to the rocks, his weapon cradled in his shoulder, ready to fire. As a precaution, he approached Sher Khan's prone figure from the head. In case he was alive, it would take him time to turn and engage.

A quick glance confirmed that Sahira was past help and he avoided looking at her again. He just hoped death for her had been instantaneous. He stood over Sher Khan, weighing up the man who had become an obsession with him. Sher Khan opened his eyes and the two men looked at each other. At that moment, Harry felt no hatred or jealousy for the doomed man. Strangely, there was no feeling of elation or gloating either. The emotion was more like scaling a challenging peak. It was over and done with and one could go home. He didn't feel the need to chat up Sher Khan or inflict pain, as he had imagined doing so many times.

Sher Khan didn't plead for mercy or feel the need for any last minute confessions. He knew his time was limited, a guest of a few more minutes in a transient life. A mujahid after all, lived by the gun and died by one. While he had courted death most of his adult life as a mujahid, he had never actually thought he would end up like this. Death happened to others and he had always seemed to be protected. His eyes were transfixed on the man who had made this happen and beaten him fair and square. Sher Khan was still looking when Harry fired. The bullet perhaps pierced the heart and for one long, shuddering breath, it seemed that Sher Khan was defying death, as he tried to raise himself, falling back immediately. The eyes were still defiant, staring at his executioner, but the light had gone out of them.

Harry sat down a little distance away on the half-constructed platform, allowing his body to relax and his mind to clear. Well, he thought, everything passes, perishes and palls in the end. In years to come, he would often regret having shot Sahira, especially after Bobby confirmed the deliberate trail of broken bangles she had left for them. He would often wonder on whose side she was on, in the end. But Harry was spared the agony of knowing he had possibly snuffed a life in the womb out, for no one knew Sahira had been pregnant and the secret died with her.

The contact was over by the time Namby arrived on the scene. He walked up to Harry, saluted and introduced himself. Then his young face split into a big grin.

'Sir,' he said. 'You were my platoon commander in the Military Academy, Sangro Company.'

'Of course,' replied Harry, getting up and shaking Namby's hand. He recalled Namby as an intelligent cadet and a Javelin throw gold medallist. 'What are you doing here?'

'I should be asking you that question sir. You have strayed into our battalion backyard,' said Namby, narrating the events till his arrival. 'But what a pity,' he kept repeating, 'to miss the action. So close and then to miss it, I just seem to be jinxed.' He walked across to examine the dead bodies, and let out a loud whistle the moment he saw Sahira.

'Wow sir,' he exclaimed. 'I didn't know there were female mujahids in the ranks. Comes as a revelation though and she's rather pretty for a fighter.'

'She is not a mujahid,' answered Harry, feeling the need to defend her. 'She is not carrying any weapons, Namby.'

'And the big guy…Who is he?' asked Namby, examining the sole of the boots. He let out a small laugh. 'Would you believe it, sir? This man went through my defended area at the LOC around this time, last year. Small world for sure!'

'His name is Sher Khan,' answered Harry, 'and he was the head of the Harkat in the Lolab.'

'This is rather bizarre!' exclaimed Namby, bending over Sahira's body and examining the gold Ganesha amulet. 'A Hindu God around the neck of a Muslim female mujahid!' He looked up sharply at Harry. 'You aren't telling the whole story here, are you sir?'

Harry laughed, 'Even in the Academy, I always thought you were too smart for this profession. Mark my words boy, either learn to act dumb when the occasion demands or perish as a superseded colonel. Leave that Ganesha around her neck Namby. I hope it brings her some luck in her next birth.' he said, wistfully. 'Now if your boys are carrying any tea rations, would you be hospitable enough to give your old instructor a cup of tea?'

Malik had run and walked non-stop. In less than an hour, he reached the ridgeline. Here he paused and looked back. Nothing was visible and the guns had fallen silent. Briefly, he mourned for his lost friend.

'Bloody women,' he muttered under his breath. 'I hope the *houri*s of *jannat* give you more happiness than that Kashmiri bitch, Sheru bhai. Go in peace to Allah, my brother. You were one of the best.'

Then turning, he hoisted his rucksack up, and went down the mountain into the swirling mist rising up from the river, beyond which lay home and safety.

Acknowledgements

At the outset a huge thanks to my course mate Mohit Malik (may his tribe increase,'The Band of Brother's') without whose perseverance this book would not be seeing the light of day. Perhaps he had more faith in my writing than I did. To Shobit the man who took a risk with the publishing—thanks a ton buddy.

Finally my gratitude to Nayantara and Nandita for the painstaking corrections—and were they plenty! And to all those unnamed well-wishers who over the years have believed I could put pen to paper.

Thank you all.

Amazon Customer Reviews

★★★★½ 4.6 out of 5 stars

A fascinating story written in superb language! It will not allow you to put down the book till it is finished. Having operated in counter-militancy operations along the Shamshabari Range and on either side of Pir Panjal Range in Jammu & Kashmir, I find the description of the terrain, locales and combat activities as authentic as can be. Only a Special Forces officer can go into such details.

—**Gen VP Malik** (Retd),
Former Chief of Army Staff

Another fascinating novel by Abhay Narayan Sapru, a third by him, that takes you through the challenges, tribulations, sweat, blood and gore of militancy and counter-insurgency in Kashmir. His characteristic inimitable style will keep you engrossed through to the last page of this narrative based on realities.

—**Lt Gen Prakash Katoch** (Retd)

THE PIR PANJAL RANGE IN KASHMIR!

Mountain stacked on mountain with the raging Chenab river meandering through. Daunting snow-clad summits, remote valleys and isolated hamlets, peopled by Muslims, Hindus and the migratory Gujjar tribesmen.The centuries-old peace between the two communities is about to be ravaged. Militancy has reared its ugly head and blood will be spilled; brother will fight brother. As the hills start burning with Pakistan-backed terror, there is vendetta being played out, with death and mayhem unleashed in its wake. Sucked into this vortex of violence and vengeance is Harry and his SF troop. Along the way, some foreign trekkers are abducted by an unknown militant group called the Al-Faran. Unbeknownst to all the dramatis-personae involved, their paths will converge violently with dire consequences for some.

The Savage Hills • Abhay Narayan Sapru
ISBN - 978-81-8328-549-0 • ₹ 395